BBC
DOCTOR WHO

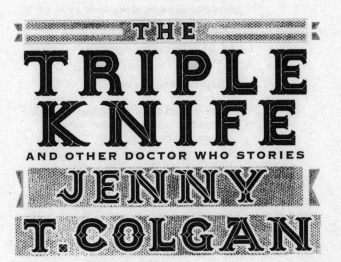

THE
TRIPLE
KNIFE
AND OTHER DOCTOR WHO STORIES

JENNY
T. COLGAN

BBC BOOKS

1 3 5 7 9 10 8 6 4 2

BBC Books, an imprint of Ebury Publishing
20 Vauxhall Bridge Road,
London SW1V 2SA

BBC Books is part of the Penguin Random House
group of companies, whose addresses can be found at
global.penguinrandomhouse.com

Penguin
Random House
UK

Doctor Who is a BBC Wales production for BBC One.
Executive producers: Steven Moffat and Brian Minchin

First published by BBC Books in 2018

www.penguin.co.uk

A CIP catalogue record for this book is available from
the British Library

ISBN 978 1 785 94371 3

Printed and bound in Great Britain by Clays Ltd, St Ives PLC

Penguin Random House is committed to a sustainable future for
our business, our readers and our planet. This book is made from
Forest Stewardship Council® certified paper.

Contents

To Russell and Steven, for guiding him safely home.

Introduction

Hello! It is a real privilege to have my stories brought together like this, particularly in *Doctor Who*'s Year of the Woman. I'm truly thrilled to have them in one place and, as it's been quite nostalgic looking back at them, I thought I'd write a short introduction as to how they came about and my thought processes as I was writing them. NB: there will definitely be some spoilers, so I'd come back and read this at the end if I were you.

The first story I wrote was 'Into the Nowhere'. I wrote it after my novel *Dark Horizons* came out and, like many new *Doctor Who* writers, I'd been thinking about it for so long that my instincts were to throw absolutely everything including the kitchen sink at it. The idea of the Nowhere planet came from *Lost*. My husband and I were addicted to the show and I was 100 per cent sure that the reason for the island was that it had the tree of forbidden fruit and at the end Jack and Kate were going to be Adam and Eve and restart the Earth. (I still like my idea better to be honest.) So 'Into the Nowhere' has gardens of Eden, snakes all over the place, some pretty cool skeleton slaves and huge writhing maggots. I really like Clara's ambivalence in the story – she was a new character when I wrote 'Into the Nowhere', and it was hard to see which side of the fence she was going to end up on. I also really like the end when the Doctor resets the weather. I had originally included a really disgusting part featuring a torture basement where people are made into skeletons, which didn't make the final cut but is still alluded to.

There's a lovely scene in Frank Cottrell-Boyce's television episode *In the Forest of the Night* featuring the TARDIS covered with ivy which always makes me think of Clara's TARDIS covered in roses at the end of 'Into the Nowhere'. The only other time the worlds of my fiction and the show have collided was in *The Boundless Sea*, an audio drama I wrote for River Song in which she wields a sonic trowel. In 'The Husbands of River Song', the Doctor notices she has a sonic trowel (yay!) but instantly says that it's 'really embarrassing', which my children, let me tell you, found absolutely hilarious.

After writing 'Into the Nowhere', *The Scientific Secrets of Doctor Who* came along, in which the *Doctor Who* stories looked at issues that were then discussed by a scientist. I was asked to look at global warming and this became 'All the Empty Towers'. I wanted to set the story in Blackpool so that Clara would recognise it; or not, as the case may be.

It was a Peter Capaldi story before the episodes had actually started airing, so I had to mostly guess what his personality would be. Gareth Roberts, who wrote *The Caretaker*, was incredibly helpful in describing how grumpy he was, certainly to begin with, and the main note was NO HUGGING, so I am very glad I got him to kiss a donkey. Also I liked the idea of a scary landlady – landladies *are* quite scary in my experience.

(I ran into Peter at an event just after I'd completed my first David Tennant audio and he asked, 'Why aren't you writing for me?' and I replied, 'I have – you have a donkey companion!' which left him slightly nonplussed.)

I wanted to set a scene in the Tower ballroom in Blackpool not realising, disappointingly, that the ballroom isn't up the tower at all. It's in the base. I recently got a chance to go there to watch my friend and fellow *Doctor Who* writer Susan Calman kick ass in *Strictly Come Dancing*, and it is far bigger and grander than I imagined, or indeed managed to convey.

'A Long Way Down' was originally a short illustrated adventure commissioned for the cover of the Time Trips collection. It was very exciting to see Ben Morris's brilliant illustrations bring it to life on the beautiful fold-out dust jacket of the original book. I needed the simplest of ideas – at one point, they got trapped in a game of marbles, but I decided to go even starker than that: the Doctor simply falls out of the TARDIS. The geraniums are of course a nod to Douglas Adams's petunias. Removed at a later stage, alas, was the fact that Clara was originally holding Seven's umbrella when she jumped. Also left out was Clara practising ballet in the TARDIS dance studio which looks out over nineteenth-century St Petersburg. I put the ballet studio back in *In the Blood* because I liked it so much.

'The Triple Knife' is barely a *Doctor Who* story at all. I had really enjoyed the Series 9 two-parter about Ashildr, the immortal girl, but the scene when we learn she lost her children to the plague was standout for me.

Nothing could be more dramatic than that. (I have three children, which probably has something to do with it.) The title refers to the fact that every time you have a child, a new sword of Damocles appears over your head: the awful horror that something might happen to them, which you then carry forever. And if you had to live forever, could it be borne? To wander endless millennia like Melmoth knowing all your children are dead feels like a torment beyond reason, and I wanted to explore those emotions.

'Picnic at Asgard' is my favourite; I think it's my most strongly realised world, even though it's not remotely frightening, unless you're a furry genetically modified raccoon named after a Roman general. I love River and put in a massive plea for 'Picnic at Asgard' when I heard that Steven was doing 'The Singing Towers of Darillium' for Christmas 2015. It's just such a huge part of the Doctor's history. We discussed doing it with the Tenth Doctor but I was against that for the simple reason that when those two meet again, all it can be about is heartache and pain, whereas I wanted them in the middle of a relationship for a very specific reason: I wanted to talk about children. River is more or less a married woman. Whether she wanted them or not, it will, at the very least, have crossed her mind.

I remember pitching it and it taking a little while and some to-ing and fro-ing before it was given the OK, and I was so very pleased when it was. I like this world, I like their relationship and I *really* like it when he wins an Olympic medal in skiing; it's sad and funny all at once. I've had more (gorgeous) fan art from this story than I have from anything else I've ever done. It's strange:

INTRODUCTION

whenever I sit on a panel someone always asks me if I don't feel constrained writing in a medium that has so much history and so many rules, and I can never quite explain how much writing *Who* has freed me up to write in any direction, and experiment in so many different ways. I suppose that's the joy of the show in the end.

Ooh, I just love writing *Doctor Who*, can't you tell? I am brimming over with excitement with the new stories and new types of stories Jodie Whittaker is going to bring to the show, as well as Chris Chibnall, the brilliant new showrunner. It is just a great time to be a woman in *Who*. And, as they well know, whenever they want me, I'll be there. With Meghan, tireless donkey companion, by my side.

The Triple Knife

August 9th 1348

And now I will write in English even though it is a language that sticks in my troat. Trout. Throat. *Alors*. So. *Donc*.

A new journal for a new journey, as there is nothing to do now except watch the rocking of the bow and listen to Essie's astonishment – my little French *enfant* – at what these English consider acceptable to serve for *dîner*.

I sang for Johann:

> *'Rough blows the North Wind... cruel blows the East...*
> *heavy blows the South Wind... we all fall BENEATH!'*

and he giggled as I tickled him under the arm, and Rue laughed because he always laughs when Johann laughs, and also he is simply one of those babies who likes to be happy; but Essie wasn't distracted at all, even as the boat pitched and rolled and we clung on to the rough wooden bench so hard I took a splinter.

Instead she looked up, away from the food, with that look on her thin face and glint in her dark eyes that I recognised immediately, and I realised I was in for an 8-year-old's inquisition, which is as relentless as a witch hunt, and I know a bit about those.

'*Maman?*'

'Mm?'

'Why did we leave Marseille again?'

'In English, please.'

She sighed crossly and repeated the question in that clunky, phlegm-ridden tongue I have painstakingly been teaching them all.

'Well, I told you. We are going to the greatest city in the world! The largest city since Rome! For adventures.'

Essie pouted. 'And why isn't Papa coming?'

'Because Papa is going to look after the fishing nets all safely for us until we have had enough adventures, and then I will send you home,' I said, because it was true.

I had… what is the good English phrase, there, I know it: I had sworn *blind*, never again, but… oh, but Tomas had been. Well.

So handsome I never saw, and he such a quiet man, practically silent. Never asked a question. Never fussed me. No curiosity about why I had a crown in my locked chest, or why, if he or I woke for any reason in the night my sword would be in my hand and at his throat before you could say, 'It was just the thunder, Alys, get back to sleep.'

As for the babies coming, the stupidity was all mine, and then there was Essie, and suddenly, from the second those tiny ageless eyes opened on my breast, sweetness and happiness was mine too, for the first time: a surprise, as I had always considered babies simply an irritating burden, like ringworm, or immortality, or frostbite.

And so I told myself Johann and Rue were essential really; so they could protect and comfort each other when I had to leave them. As, one day I will. As I have to leave everyone as they turn curious, then suspicious, then horrified, then superstitious and finally murderous, and I think, well, my own children could not do that, but I have seen children do things to parents too, terrible things, because I have seen everything, and I know I could not bear it.

And so we are leaving Tomas, so that even my quiet man cannot say one more time, it's astonishing, truly, is it not strange that three babies and twenty years have not marked you, no, not an inch, and does your hair not grow?

August 10th

The bark creaked. I paid a lot of gold for this tide. Thank goodness it turned early, before Tomas had even stirred. Essie disappeared, and I found her behind a heaped chest of shining oranges, bent over in concentration.

'What are you doing now?'

I have no fear of the other sailors as a woman alone: they are good enough men on the whole, and I made a point of standing on the prow first day and juggling knives. I pretended it was to entertain the littles, but when I threw them under the boson's legs and caught them without looking, glinting in the sun, I believe they got the message more or less.

'Ugh,' said Essie. 'They served pig gruel for breakfast.'

'The food is different in Britain to France.'

'You should tell them,' she said. 'Pig food is for pigs and please may we have some human food please thank you very much also tea.'

She is obsessed with this new idea of tea. I smiled as the greasy-faced boy who acts as 'cook', if you could call it that, overheard this and grimaced and I distracted her quickly.

'I liked it,' said Johann quietly, hiding behind my skirts. It's true, he likes everything, and I caressed his curly head.

'Well, you shall make a fine strong English lad,' I said and he smiled and stuck his tongue out at his sister.

'Look, *Maman*!' said Essie, ignoring her little brother.

It was then I noticed the rat in the dim corner, bigger than a kitten. He was an ugly brute, but I was pleased to see him. When you can't find a rat: that's the time to worry about a ship.

'Don't touch him,' I said. 'He might bite you.'

She showed me a small piece she must have prised off the wheel of good Nederlander cheese I brought wrapped in a cloth.

'He likes this.'

'I expect he does. He likes fingers too.'

'You won't eat me, will you Rose?' said Essie, leaning towards the rat, who hissed.

'Rose?'

'It's a pretty name.'

I looked at her. 'I suppose it is. But don't let it get too close.'

It was too late. The rat was already nibbling from her fingers because, one, Essie disobeys everything I ask her to do as a matter of principle, and two, she loves all creatures, animals, the weaker and the younger the better. She always has. I know I should teach her to stay away from the weak; to seek out the strong and close her ears to everyone else. I've seen it time and time again; it's the only way not to stumble by the wayside. But it doesn't matter; I can't change her. And in truth I don't want to. She is the very, very best of me.

'There you are, Rose! Nice and delicious, yum yum yum!'

I realised Essie was now giving her lunch to her rat. He didn't seem to like it much either.

I glanced over to where a couple of the sailors were tossing Rue in the air to make him giggle. He's become quite the pet. Johann was watching enviously, and so I went over and grabbed him impulsively, clambered up the steps out of the musty below decks and onto the foredeck, where the spray was lighting the air, so fresh and salty it made you gasp, and the little bark was tossing down and up, but none of us gets sick easily; and instead I swung Johann round and round as he giggled and his little hands grabbed my shoulders and I twirled him into the netting, just as someone shouted, 'Land ahoy!'

I stopped whirling Johann, who shouted, 'More, more!' and instead stopped and smelled the cool earth as we glided into the deep mouth of a river; someone said 'South of Hamp Town', and people on the wide, wide beaches stopped from what they were doing – gathering eels in their nets, the midshipman told me – and looked up. There were cooking fires dotted across the bone-white sand, and they looked like tiny stars.

August 13th

'Why is it so big, *Maman*? Who are all these people? They are dressed strangely.'

'You have a lot of opinions for an 8-year-old.'

'In Marseille, they have silk,' Essie had returned serenely, as we finally reached our lodgings, beating off the clamouring hands of the young grubby boys who had accosted us at every town shouting, 'Lodgings? Safe! Clean! Carry your bags,' despite the fact you could see the lice dance on them even as they spoke.

'And also it is almost mostly definitely not raining at home,' said Essie.

'Look up,' I said.

The houses fell against each other like weary travellers – many timbered, two-storeyed, collapsed drunks, shop signs creaking in the breeze. And above them were the great stained-glass windows of the cathedral, their colours holding an exhausted Johann in its spell. Also, the longer they looked up at the great church, the less time they spent looking at the iron poles with the remains of traitors on them, and the crows that perched there.

I have been to Trondheim, and to Paris, so I consider myself knowing in the ways of cities, but this place is different altogether; so vast, so filled with different people, so empty of anyone who would give us a second glance amongst the rowdy jugglers, the shouting sellers, the mendicants, the soldiers and the priests, of course. Always the priests.

I kept all our clothes plain to avoid notice as we pushed through the throng, but I had enough gold sewn into the lining of my cloak to find us decent lodgings near the Moor's Gate, far enough away I thought from the stench of the tanneries, but I was wrong about that.

Essie was quiet and tired after the long journey, and I felt nauseous myself. We were long enough in the cart, next to a French woman, Madame Bellice, who kept her nose buried in a bouquet of lavender that reminded me of Provence, and protested that the English stank of old milk. Johann burbled to her in French but she was indefatigably uncharmed, then Essie started being rude about her in English and required a scolding I did not truly mean and kept smirking through.

It served me right when I turned up to our new lodgings and found she was lodged just across the street. I don't care. I don't make friends.

The road bustled full of people making their way to or from the smarter merchants' homes, leading donkeys laden with meat, fish I could already tell would not be welcome, spices I had not smelled in years and bolts of cloth, all colours. I had to tug Johann away from the spectacle that was simply daily city life.

We entered our new home, which had straw, clean enough, on the ground; a clear fireplace and a bed for us all and a cot for the baby. I have seen rather worse.

Essie was looking pale and white, and I grabbed a pot from my bag just in time as she threw up into it.

'I'm not sure you're the best traveller,' I said, then I got distracted by something squirming under her sack.

'You didn't bring Rose?'

She looked up at me, her brown eyes absolutely huge in her heart-shaped face. 'She's my friend, *Maman*,' she said. 'I'm sure she didn't like living on that boat.'

The rat regarded me malevolently.

'I'm sure she didn't,' I said. 'But there are enough rats in this town already.'

'Please can we keep her?' Essie's eyes were rimmed with pink. The rat was biting furiously at the handkerchief she'd tied him in.

'Darling, get some rest,' I said. 'We'll see in the morning.'

'That means no!' said Essie, in that confused fury of extremely fatigued children. '"We'll see" always means "No"!'

'Get some rest,' I said shortly. Rue didn't look well either. And of course that rat will be long gone in the morning, hopefully a poor man's breakfast.

I stepped outside to dispose of Rose, who suffered at the end of my sword a cleaner death than most of my enemies.

At the corner of our lane, I heard a commotion and moved closer to the wall. It is my new aim: to avoid confrontation. I've seen enough of fighting, I think. Surely. For now.

To my surprise it was Madame Bellice, the lady from the carriage and now our neighbour. She was screaming and yelling, and a thick crowd had of course gathered round, but nobody would go near her.

'Look at me!' she was screaming. 'Find me a physician.'

I glanced through the crowd. She was holding up her hands and screaming in pain. Large black growths were visible underneath her arms. The women in the crowd were running away with their children. Suddenly she saw me.

'Madame! Madame! Alys! *Aidez-moi!* Help me!' she cried, sweat running off her, her eyes completely wide in terror.

'I have children,' I said, but her face was so desperate I approached, telling Johann, who trots everywhere after me like a puppy, to stay back.

'I am so sick,' she said. 'Please, please, find me a physician, a doctor.'

'Is there a doctor?' I said to the crowd, but nobody turned round or identified themselves.

'It's the plague!' shouted one man suddenly and the crowd gasped. I heard rumours of plague too, coming up from the Nubians, but had not seen it. Surely it was not here.

'She's got the plague! God have mercy on us!'

A cold hand clutched my heart. She was in our carriage. Or, we were in hers.

Instantly the people dispersed, running, some of them. It was fun, apparently, watching the crazy lady, but the diseased lady, that's a little too much.

I hissed at Johann to stay by our doorway on the other side of the street. I was about to leave when I heard a heartrending sob come from Madame Bellice.

Ach. Motherhood has ripped a layer of skin right off me. She was sobbing exactly like Johann did when Essie broke his wooden dog by washing it in the river; as if the world would end.

I sighed. I already knew not much can harm me.

I led her inside her lodgings, which were much like ours, and laid her down. Her room was heavy with sweat, waste and disease. I looked around for clean straw for her bed, but there was none, so I laid the least dirty rug down instead.

'Lie down and I'll go to the well for you,' I said in French. 'You have to boil the water.' I learned this trick on the silk route, from a Japanese woman almost older than I am, and it has not failed me yet.

'It hurts so much,' she said, wild eyed and thrashing. 'Make it stop! Make it stop!'

'I'll try and find someone to help,' I said, looking around, although this woman had the stink of death on her, and once it begins, it is a timely fool's errand to try and reverse it.

I turned to leave to fetch the water, but suddenly there was a shadow cast through the sun of morning; an ominous shape appeared in the doorway. It startled me.

It was a man, but wearing a strange mask, like the huge beak of a bird, in some sort of leather. He also wore a broad hat fanning out from his head, and a long cloak, all in the same material. He reminded me of the crows I had seen at Traitor's Gate.

I stepped forward. 'Yes?'

'I am a Scientist,' stated the figure in a strange, accent-less voice. I had not heard this word before. I stepped back.

'Are you the physician? Can you help?'

'I will examine. It will help.'

'No,' said the Madame, suddenly terrified and shrinking away from him. And it was true: the man had a sinister countenance.

'This is the doctor come. He can help you,' I said, although I was not sure about either of these things.

The figure came forward, opening a black bag he had with him. He had a strange gait. 'Let me examine you.'

Suddenly outside I could hear Essie screaming '*Maman! Maman!* I'm sick again!' I froze as icy water cascaded through my heart.

'I have to go,' I said.

The figure continued to approach. Something struck me as strange about him, but I couldn't tell what it was, and was too torn to care.

'Don't leave me,' begged the woman in a guttural tone. 'Don't leave me.'

Outside Essie shouted my name once more.

'I have to,' I said and backed away. 'Good luck. Look after her,' I commanded the medicine man, who opened his big black bag full of instruments, like a dentist, or a surgeon or a butcher, and did not respond.

And I left and ran to Essie and picked her up in my arms and took her home, just as Madame Bellice began to scream.

August 15th

August 16th

Oh, the fevered days and endless nights, no better for knowing I cannot be relinquished, for I would have willingly been relinquished.

August 17th

August 18th

The soldiers came this morning. But it was my least bad night: the buboes were shrinking, the children slept, finally, wiped out, but sleeping, and I thought, 'We are through; we are finally through this.'

I had made us drink lots of water boiled over the fire, trying to force the sickness from our bodies and finally this morning, although I was exhausted, I was almost better and could stand. The children seemed better too, and I was heating up some oats for our breakfast and wondering if all the bread in London was mealy and black or if the town warranted more investigation, when I heard a pike at the door. I recognised it immediately.

'Open up!' called the soldier.

I rolled my eyes. I thought we had been through enough in London town. 'Yes, yes, right away, just coming,' I shouted back cheerily.

I hushed the children and quickly took out my knife. Whatever they required, if there's one thing I've learned about soldiers it's this: getting captured is the first mistake. I am not the spoils of war.

Always move first. If he thinks he's listening for a woman who'll be cowering back protecting her children, then he'll have another think coming.

'Open. . .'

I hurled the door open with my foot and whacked my knife up against the side of his neck, holding it there before he had a chance to notice what had happened, and kicked the pike out of his hand. It clattered onto the muddy street.

'What do you want?'

'Unhand me.'

His fellow came round from the other side. 'Put the knife down!' he commanded.

He expected me to turn my face in his direction and answer him. So I did not do this; instead, I darted out quick as a snake and tripped him in the mud, ramming my foot somewhere I knew it would hurt.

'NOW!' I shouted. 'ANSWER ME!'

So. It turns out England is not in the least like the Hundred Years War, and they have all these rule of law things and everything.

I was locked up in a white tower, with a broken toe and the usual cuts and bruises, which didn't bother me in the slightest, even though one of the gaolers looked slightly shamefaced at locking up a lady; whereupon he tried to handle the tile around my neck and I shoved him away.

So I am locked up fairly comprehensively, even by my standards. (I have checked for the usual: wall coverings for ladders; bars I can squeeze through; persuadable guards, so far without joy. They didn't look even tempted. Perhaps everything I have heard about English men is true.)

A rather charming *gentilhomme* called Godfroi came to interview me; he had the nose of a hawk, and a profile that could only be English; his neck sloping straight down from the chin; a soft voice that did not need to shout to bring authority, for who in England does not know their estate?

They tied me to a chair in a windowless torture dungeon with a fire roaring, although it is summer time, and an array of pokers and pliers to scare me, which cheered me mightily as both make excellent weapons, and they had left me with none.

The man coughed. 'So you are newly arrived, and you are accused of spreading the sickness.'

'Why would I move to a country and try to kill everybody in it?'

The man shrugged. 'In my experience that is precisely what foreigners do.'

I folded my arms. 'Well, it's not true. I've had it myself.'

The man coughed again. At first I thought he simply had the pallid flesh of his countrymen. Now I realised he himself was pale and sickening, fast.

'Half your street is dead. And it is carrying on. But you, we see, are not dead. Did you do this by witchcraft? Can you stop it?'

'Is this a trial? I have my own ducking stool.'

'Bringing sickness is punishable by death,' he said, coughing again.

I glanced at the instruments by the fire. He saw me looking and beckoned over his guards to stand closer. Two guards. I turned my gaze away in case he saw in my eyes that two dozen might just about give us a fair fight.

On the other hand there was a moat to swim and locks to navigate and I was very tired and anxious to get home to my littles.

'There are physicians,' I said suddenly. 'There was a doctor on the street.'

He looked up. 'What kind of a doctor?'

'They say they do science. They can fix things.'

'Where were they from?'

'I couldn't tell. They were wearing masks.'

'Fools and tricksters,' he said. 'Preying on the sick and the stupid.'

'Maybe,' I said.

He looked at me, his pale eyes curious. And something else. Desperate.

They left me in the torture chamber for a long time. Certainly long enough to loosen my bonds. So much for the most feared prison in England. I once spent a season getting tied up every night by a young monk in a flagellant's monastery in Amiens. We both learned a lot that year.

'Essie knows how to get to the well,' I thought. 'Please, please, please, let her remember to boil the water.'

Godfroi returned as I heard guards tramping back in, cross and empty-handed. They had found no strange physicians; just legions and legions of the dead or nearly dead.

I realised then I simply had to leave. My three chicks needed me.

'Sorry. . .' I leaned over as Godfroi entered. 'I shouted but nobody would respond. . . but I remembered one other thing they said about where they were going to be. . . I'm so, so sorry not to have mentioned it before. . .' My tone was conversational and light and I leaned forward to talk in a conciliatory manner with the visibly weakening interrogator. 'I think they said they were going to be in—'

I kicked out my chair and brought up my knee, which made the table ricochet off his bent-forwards forehead, practically knocking him out.

The guards jumped towards me but I grabbed a poker and a set of tongs in either hand and, bang, threw my arms up on either side like I wished to fly. They both went reeling and I grabbed Godfroi, removed his knife, and hauled him towards the door. He looked almost relieved someone was propping him up; he weighed almost nothing. Not only that, but he didn't pull away or resist me in any way. I gave him an enquiring glance.

'If I'm your prisoner,' he said weakly, 'will you take me to see these doctors?'

'Yes,' I said grimly.

'Let her pass,' he whispered hoarsely to the other guards who were gathering on the stairs. 'I am her hostage and her powers are legion. Let us pass I command you.'

We burst down the stairs and onto the bright street, and I hailed a boatman to take us up river. He took us without commenting on the knife I held, although he did mew that he could not go further than Aldgate at this time of day and I said, 'You will,' and used Godfroi's sword to rip open the hem of my coat, and scattered the gold within on the prow.

The street was quiet, and I tore towards my door, the man in tow.

'*Maman!*' came a voice and I nearly screeched in relief and joy and pulled Essie, pale, so thin, into my arms and whirled her around.

'I took good care of Rue,' she whispered, and I wiped his precious brow and hoisted him onto the sling on my back, which had felt so empty, and Johann clung to me with filthy dirty fingers and my heart burst with joy, and I gave gold to Essie and told her to go to the bakers and buy every sweetmeat they had.

'Set me down,' said Godfroi. I had forgotten all about him; he was leaning against a wall, breathing heavily; he could have run away a hundred times and I would not have cared a whit, but here he was, panting, diminished so.

I let him lie on my good rug, which shows I am not evil in fact. Johann padded over and patted the man on his strange pale hair and looked up at me questioningly.

'Is he our new friend?'

'Hmm,' I said.

Essie came slowly back from the bakers with a few tired cakes in her basket. 'No more cakes,' she said sadly. 'The lady said no more cakes, for the baker is dead.'

I looked for the cheerful words I could put on this and found none, except that, like me, thank goodness the children appeared to be over the sickness and thus immune, like their measles and their quinsy. So I put out the stale honey cakes anyway.

'These taste old, *Maman*,' complained the little gourmande, after one bite.

'I like them,' said Johann, looking at me hopefully for praise. I let the baby suck on one; let his gummy paws sticky as a cub in honey whilst I tended to Godfroi on the floor, grateful that my children were past the danger.

'Water?'

25

But he couldn't keep a thing down and I turned my head as I felt, rather than saw, the shadow at the door.

This time there were three of them, all the same size and shape, with those great pointed beaks on their faces.

They moved smoothly and slowly and I realised what it was that was so strange about them: they did not smell as we did.

They did not smell of England or of the North or of France or everywhere I had been on Earth: of blood; old straw, of livestock, of the latrines we trod through every day in rivulets on the streets; of the old food and fetid cheese and turned meat we ate in town, or the curds of country living; the special smell of gaps of teeth in the mouth, the ancient salty sweat from clothing never removed and cuts undressed: the proper, natural rich and loamy deep smell of all the things that live.

They smelled of a place I had been once before, a long time ago; a clean, empty space without muck or soil. Oh yes. I had smelled it before.

A spaceship.

I could scarce remember the word. But oh, my body remembered, for my eyes started blinking rapidly, and my heart pounded, and I felt a feeling of battle soak through my veins.

These men... they came from those places beyond the stars. I looked at their masks again. I did not see straps, or joins. Were they even masks at all?

I stepped forward. But were they friends, like the girl in the box? Or false friends, like the man in the box? Or destroyers, like Odin?

And if they were friends... My heart leapt again. No more trying to scratch a living day by day. We could go, out into that wild universe where creatures such as me were not unknown; where there were lives we could have where I did not lie; where I did not have to give up my children and pretend to be unknown to them; where I was not unnatural; where I did not have to lie and kill and cheat every day of my life simply to get by.

I stepped forward. 'Here they are,' I said to Godfroi, whose pallid face had taken on a hopeful look as they entered.

Johann stood behind me. 'Scared, *Maman*! Bad men!'

'Not to you,' I whispered carefully, keeping my eyes on them.

The Scientists took out a sharp implement with something I had not seen for a long, long time: a light that was not fire.

Once again, excitement lit up my breast. Johann forgot his shyness and came out to gaze upon the tool in wonder. Essie looked at me, happy and excited like she was at a travelling fayre. The instrument gave out a beam of violet light that crossed the room.

Oh yes. I had seen lights like that before. Lights from other worlds, other places.

'Don't touch it,' I said, feeling Rue's grabby fingers behind me. 'Don't!'

I hastily unbundled Rue and shoved him into Essie's arms. I had to see what was happening, but they did not.

'All of you. Outside,' I said. 'Outside, now.'

Essie opened her mouth to protest, but for once she listened to me. It was Johann who was transfixed by the lights and I had to push him sharply through the open doorway, although it pained me to do so. 'Go!'

There was a hissing noise as the beam of light started to travel across the floor.

'You see,' I said boldly to the Scientists, 'I have a proposition for you. For where you came from...'

I had no idea what my proposition actually was, but I felt we had to start somewhere. All three ignored me, however, their beaks following the path of the light, and the man on the floor.

'Help me!' moaned Godfroi in supplication.

And then, in an instant, all was whited out in a scream as the travelling light entered his shoulder and carried on, until the arm fell, with a thump, clean off on the floor and then even the scream was cut off, as he quickly dropped into a merciful faint as the light somehow stopped the wound from bleeding – I could not tell why nor how.

'What are you?' I said, rushing to Godfroi's side, even as one of the figures picked up the discarded arm and started examining the black lumps on it. He cut through the arm quickly and efficiently, as the other man came up with strange black bags that, I now realised, buzzed and moved as they were filled.

'What are you? What are you doing?' I said.

One glanced at me. 'We are Scientists,' he said.

'You said that. I don't know what the word means.'

'We discover things. We test things. We work on things that are harmful and make cures.'

'Are you going to cure the plague?'

The masked man nodded his head. 'Yes,' he said. 'But not here.' He looked around. 'We examine, we dissect.

We take back evidence and information to stop our own people from getting sick. Far, far from here.'

'How far?' I breathed.

On the floor, Godfroi was stirring. His body was jerking and racked with pain. Even though he was a gaoler and a torturer, I still did not like to see it. And especially not on my rug.

'Can't you cure him?'

'Why?' said the Scientist dispassionately. 'He is not us. You too should use other animals to test your sicknesses on.'

I stared at him, puzzled. 'That's inhuman.'

'Correct. We are not human.'

'Are you...' I glanced out of the window at the suddenly deathly quiet streets that only a few days ago had been so crowded and choked with the colour of humanity; at Godfroi, moaning and writhing on the floor. This world... all I have seen of this world with its wars and its death and pointless cruelty... Oh, it feels done for me.

'Are you leaving now? To travel back to your own people?'

'When we have the samples we need.'

'Can...' I swallowed. 'Can we come with you?'

Wherever they go, I thought, it cannot be worse than traipsing so painfully slowly through the muck of this world.

They stopped, all three, together. Their beaks turned towards each other, curious. 'No disease carriers on the ship,' said one. 'Customs controls.'

'But an entire specimen,' said one. 'And it is free from disease. What could we not learn from it?'

'Patient Zero,' said the other.

They advanced towards me. I stayed stock still, as the huge beaks turned, and then sniffed loudly in my direction.

'A perfect specimen. What could we not infect her with?'

Their voices were rising in excitement.

'We could try everything. . . from someone as healthy as our own population!'

'And my children,' I said boldly.

Their beaks bobbed up and down excitedly. 'Better and better with the younglings. Are they all in good health?'

'There will. . . there will be experiments,' said the third, sealing his black bag with Godfroi's diseased arm in it.

I blinked. We would see about that. They could not hold me. I knew it. Nothing can.

And once we were free – away, in space, in the planets, in the many planets beyond this world – and I know there are legion, for I have sat, many, many nights, in the coldest mountains and the hottest deserts and I have tried to count them, and I cannot – I could fight, I could break them. They would not hold me. I would escape and be free, all of us together, riding the stars for ever.

'Take me.'

They were decided.

'We will take you.'

'Essie! Johann!' I shouted outside. 'Come. Our journey continues.'

'*BON!*' shouted Essie without hesitation, my bold girl.

And I knelt down and covered Godfroi, who was very near the end now. 'I'm sorry,' I said. 'I have to leave.'

He opened his pale terrified eyes. 'You, Dame of Misfortune. You brought this.'

'Nobody knows what brought it.'

'Will there. . . Do you think Hell is waiting for me?'

'Somewhere worse than Earth?' I said. 'I doubt it.'

'Let's go!' said Essie, bundling up her clothes. 'What is their food like?'

'Have they got big lights?' said Johann, his eyes wide. 'I like the big lights!'

We followed the figures outside. How strange to see the city deserted, from the great town houses, made of stone, to the lowliest hovel; everywhere, nothing but crosses on the doors, and quiet sobbing, a low field of lament, almost too quiet to hear, and a deep, lone voice, coming from far away: 'Bring out! Bring out your dead!'

But I was not sure there was anyone left here to bring out the dead, and they could not walk.

Behind the deserted baker's, its shingle tumbling down, we saw it, tucked in a stable; something black and shiny. In the shadows it was almost invisible, but as we got closer we saw it was a pointed ship, and we saw that it shone, that it was a strange metal I had never seen before.

'Ohhh!' said Johann and the baby on my back pointed out his little sticky finger.

'It's beautiful,' I said.

'You are ours,' they said.

'You think that,' I smiled politely.

The great door opened silently, lowered a plank, like a ship's, to the floor. My heart exulted. Inside was full of lights, as well as specimen boxes; an examination table and many other pieces of equipment I did not recognise. Some of it would work perfectly well as weapons. We were so ready.

'STOP!'

I turned at the noise. I should not have done.

It was Godfroi, stumbling, lurching, his remaining arm turning him into a travesty, his teeth bared like that of a man already dead. 'You did this to us!' he shouted, screamed at me. 'You came and infected us all.'

'No I didn't.'

'You are a Dame of Misfortune, I could see it all along.'

He was deranged. Best simply to leave.

'Let's go,' I said, quickly, to the bird men. 'Let's just go.'

Essie was almost at the gangplank. The baby was with me. Where was...

I turned round. Too late. Too late.

'Bye, friend,' my little curly-haired Johann was saying, right up at him. And Godfroi had him by the neck, and was starting to squeeze with his black and pustuled arm.

'You shall not keep him, Dame of Misfortune! And let all the misfortunes become yours!'

I trained for many years so none can best me on the field of battle. I am strong as ten men, through careful work; I can shoot an arrow through a bee and fell a dragoon. I have made myself the greatest fighter the world has ever known.

But that does not matter for this reason: the weakest, feyest mother ever born would have done without hesitation what I did next. In an instant. For that is simply what being a mother is.

I slew him with one clean blow of his own sword. The bird men looked on, silently. Johann was wiping his neck where that man had grabbed him, as Godfroi's blackened corpse dropped to the ground like an emptied sack, and I was glad.

I took Johann in my arms, although he was by rights getting too big to be lifted. Still nobody moved.

The bird man slowly sniffed the air with his huge beak. He brought up his large gloved hand and he pointed, steadily and slowly at Johann. Everyone stopped. Silence fell.

'That one,' he said. 'That one is still sick.'

'No,' I said. 'No, no, he's fine. He's had it. He's fine.'

Even as I could feel my beautiful boy's curls were stuck with sweat to his head.

'No living carriers,' said the other, pulling out his pointed light device. He flicked it on. My little boy was half worried, half delighted to see the light again.

'*Maman!*'

I froze, utterly horrified by what was unfolding in front of me. The shapes advanced on my boy.

But not for long. I grabbed Godfroi's filthy sword, and launched myself at the bird-like creature, a word on my tongue that was not French and not English but more ancient and coarse than both.

And I plunged it straight into the first beaked creature, without a thought for consequence or a thought at all except the blackest, bloodiest rage I had ever conceived of.

It was as I had perhaps suspected, but could not bring myself to believe: his leather-like garments were not leather, but instead his skin, tough as steel. I could not get purchase.

The other Scientists, though, did not come to his aid; they stood back, coolly observing, as the first thrashed his arm about – his strength was extraordinary – and suddenly his fingers uncoiled from what I had thought were gloves; they were in fact three times as long, like tentacles waving from his wrist, each pointed and sharp, and one pierced me in the chest like a needle, and I felt it as it started to draw blood from my body.

I screeched, and Essie grabbed Rue and ran back to the house, but Johann leapt forward and bit the Scientist hard on the leg, even as I screamed at him to stop, and that was just enough to startle the beast, and gave me enough time to jump back and pull out the needle, whereupon I swung my shoulders, as hard and as strongly as I ever had done anything; every second of training, every moment of battle was in it, as well as every ounce of fury that anyone would dare – *dare* – declare any of my children to be less than perfect, and I screamed and grunted and hacked and swore all the curses, and the arm of the Scientist, still twitching, the tentacles bouncing and open, was lying flat on the ground and he made a sound as crows do, when I shoot them from the trees with my bow without a second thought.

There was a terrible long silence settling in the tiny end of the baker's lane. I sensed sickening faces at windows. Then, from the Scientist I had wounded, more shrieking.

'Hellllp mmeeee,' he said, his huge head twisting, confused, as if he were trying to pick up his arm with the arm he no longer had.

I stood back, waiting, panting, but with my sword still held high. It was not covered in blood; rather something more glutinous and transparent.

'Helllp meeee.'

The first Scientist simply picked up the light pointer and immediately started to dissect the hand on the ground. The other brought his black bag, for taking back samples.

'Helllp meeee.'

The one with the light turned towards the Scientist on the ground. 'Now we shall examine the effects of pain on the spinal cortex.'

'Nooooo!'

'Stop!' I said.

'But this is Science,' they said.

Their injured comrade was now on the ground, contorted in pain. I knelt down by him.

'Our job is to rid our planet of disease,' he stuttered.

I nodded. 'By experimenting on others,' I said. 'So much for you.'

The buzzing of the light intensified. It was approaching.

'Tell me. Why do you think Johann is sick?' I said fiercely.

'I smell it,' said the Scientist. 'That is our beaks. We sniff out disease and injury and we work out how to stop it.'

'But you kill the person you experiment on?'

'Sometimes that is how Science works.'

'Didn't you think it was wrong?'

'Science has no right or wrong; only what is true.'

I blinked. 'What is wrong with Johann? He has had the sickness. He can't get it now.'

He shook his head. 'This disease doesn't work like that. This is something you can keep getting.'

I shook my head. 'But they seem better.'

The bird eyes blinked. 'They are trying to do their best. For you. But they are dead already.'

The light buzzed louder.

'As I am,' he said.

I lowered my head. 'What is it?'

'It is a simple disease. Carried by fleas, on rats.'

I shot up. Essie's rat. Godfroi had been right, curse him. 'No.'

'Don't leave me. Don't let me die alone.'

'You are not alone,' I said. 'You have your perfect brethren to tend you.'

The two other Scientists approached, and bent over him, with their needles and equipment and black bags; like doctors, yes. But much more like carrion crows.

I hurried back to our cottage. And there I saw that I should no longer fool myself. All the honey cakes, still there. Unfinished; barely touched. Sitting accusingly in a row. What child does not eat a honey cake, however old? Only a very, very sick one.

They were huddled together on the straw together; scared, as if they had done something wrong.

'*Maman*,' said Essie, quietly.

I stared at them; took in the stench of death that had settled; the stench all around of this godforsaken mud hole of a world and felt the end of everything;

for everything I try is bad and wrong and gets worse; nothing will change, nothing will ever get better for me. And I am so tired of it, again and again and again, and I will not stand for it. No more. No.

NO.

Blinded, I ordered them to nap, then charged back outside, round the corner. The gleaming ship was still parked there. Of the first scientist there was almost nothing left; they had chopped him up and packed him away. But I didn't care about that, I did not care about him. I had absolutely nothing left to lose.

This entire filthy world had sickened and died on me. But I still had my knife and my sword.

'You must still take me,' I said boldly. 'To the stars.'

'Of course,' said one. 'We are always happy to have bodies donated to medical science.'

The two Scientists marched up their gangplank without looking behind them.

I looked behind at the once-bustling, now empty streets of a town I had barely got to know; where I had, running once again to escape, found nothing but the very bile of life.

Inside the ship, a buzz and a hum had started up and lights had started to sparkle inside the cabin in the most remarkable fashion, and the excitement built up in me, that finally, FINALLY I could leave it all behind me.

Yes of course I had loved them, but they were dead. They were dead.

'Wait for me!'

I will always remember this from the many battlefields I have traversed when the young men fell.

Whether French or Saxon or Nordic, their last words were always the same and they weren't, I should say, much about poetry, or death and glory and the magnificence of battle and their wonderful rewards in the afterlife.

As I stepped across the red fields and the bodies of the dying time after time wiping my blade, I heard them say only one thing, in different tongues: mother. *Mummy. Maman. Mutter. Madre, o Madre.*

They all, at the end, cried out for their mothers, like the little boys they were, with their big steel hats and their scarlet cloaks and their fancy horses.

You will all die, except for me.

You may die on the field of battle, or retching black bile helplessly in a room that reeks of the tannery, or without your mind in your own filth in a corner, staring at long ago.

There are no noble deaths. And most people – oh, you are so, so alone. So alone.

When you came into this world there were warm arms to greet you, to welcome you and hold you, to take you, and make you feel a part of this world, hold your flesh to the flesh whence you came; still your cries to the soft motion of your mother's heartbeat as she held you in her arms and promised over and over again how she would love you for as long as the moon and the stars.

But the moon and the stars are cold and do not care and last for ever. And when you leave the world, when you are undone, you will be alone: ripped on a foreign field, or under the hooves of a galloping horse, or sweating your life blood out, or babbling to yourself on a chair, the world disdaining to come near you, to warm your pallid, sinking flesh.

And you will want your mother.

I looked at the beautiful – and it was so, so beautiful, gleaming bright shiny metal – I looked at the beautiful ship once more.

The Scientists inside looked back at me, and cocked their strange heads.

The stink in our little home is deep now; the end is close. Rue is crying his little lungs out, but plaintively, not demanding; not in a way he thinks anyone will hear him. Essie is breathing in a shallow way, but trying to say, 'Rue, Rue, don't cry.' Johann simply stares at me, his eyes huge and mute in terror.

I feel once more around my neck. The tile is there of course. It is always there. The tile that shares immortality. Waiting to be given. I look from face to face.

I have tried to cut it. I have sharpened my knife, so many times. It will not cut. It cannot be shared.

Will it be my brave, my brilliant Essie? My sweet, my loving Johann? Or my laughing baby, whom I do not even know?

And then I think, 'It cannot be the baby. He would be a baby for ever.' And I look at my girl and my boy. And my heart, which has been kicked from palace to ditch, from shore to shore, is stabbed anew. And I am looking at my girl and my boy. My girl and my boy.

I step forward, lifting the tile up and away from my body. I tear my eyes away from my beautiful tousle-headed boy, who is gazing at me. I cannot. I cannot look at him. I take one more step towards Ess, my skin crawling with horror at what I am about to do.

Then suddenly Essie groans in deep pain. And I freeze and shudder. I do not know how this alien magic I carry works, nor what it is supposed to do.

What if. . . what if it freezes her, not just as a child, but as a sick child? What if it keeps her in this foul state for ever? Could one imagine a worse torture?

My hand flies to my mouth in horror. I stare at the tile. I was in good health when he did what he did to me.

Oh, for all the times I have been tried as a witch: if I only could, truly, curse the man who did this to me, if I could pull his blood out across the stars, slowly, drop by drop whilst he screamed the heavens apart, then I would.

I let the tile fall slowly back against my skin and heave a great sigh.

'*Maman?*' says Essie, her voice trembling.

I sit on the damp straw bed, pick up the baby, who quietens immediately and nuzzles into my neck, the way his head is designed to fit so perfectly there. And I gather Johann in one crook of my elbow, and Essie just about manages, pale and weary as she is, to lie on the other.

'What's happening?' says Essie, as weak as if she is waking from a dream.

'You are going. . .' I say. 'On a journey. Like on the boat. But where you are going there will be no sickness and no pain.'

'Will you be with us, *Maman*?' says Johann, croaking. His little hands are pinned tightly around my waist.

I take the deepest of breaths. 'Listen to me. I will be with you every single second. My arms will be around you and I will be loving you and you will never ever think for a second of your life that you were not utterly beloved, every single bit of you, everything you ever were from the moment I knew you were coming; everything you ever did, everything you ever were or could ever be, was wonderful and perfect in my eyes. You were so beloved, and you made me so very, very happy. The happiest I have ever been in my whole life, and the happiest I will ever be, and I am so very, very proud of you and I am always here for you, every single second.'

His little face relaxes and he smiles. 'Was I good?'

'You were so very much better than good.'

'I am so tired, *Maman*.'

'Sleep a while,' I say.

The baby is already quiet. Oh, he is so very quiet. Essie's head is heavy on my arm. Her dark soft hair lies across my skin.

'Sweet *Maman*, sing,' she says, her eyelashes fluttering across her downy cheek, every freckle on it something I have made, worshipped, adored; every single beat of her, and I should, I will not regret a single moment, and the infinity of howling misery that blows the carved wooden door to eternal winter open in front of me, well, shall we say that it was worth it?

'Rough blows the North Wind, cruel blows the East'

This tiny gap of light you opened for me, you three, in my infinity of dark; that tiniest moment of sunshine:

shall we say then that the thousand thousand days of misery are worth the three cooling heads at my breast, shall we?

'Heavy blows the South Wind, we all fall beneath. . .'

Of course, of course we shall. . . it was worth it and I will pay for it willingly, every second: oh my loves, oh my loves, how you were loved how I loved.

August 24th

August 25th

August 26th

August 27th

I knotted Essie's plaited hair tight around my wrist as my warrior's totem and set out just after dawn. There was panic in the city now, you could feel it; the disease spreading everywhere. It was a beautiful morning too.

They were burying the corpses beyond the city walls. I looked in pity at the men who took this work; who provided some accompaniment, at least, at the end, when the finest and the great and rich ladies and gentlemen had fled in short order. I did not think they would escape it. Rich and poor, we all end the same, for

I have been both. Except of course I do not end. But the having of children. That has ended.

And here and there I saw shapes that startled me: the belief that the bird-men were indeed physicians has stayed strong, for those who do care, those who have agreed to help tend the sick; they now wear the great beaked masks, to show what they do.

I passed one on his way through the fields, who nodded.

'Rather you than me,' I said, for I was trying out myself anew, and feel the need now to only ever be light.

He shrugged.

'My money is on the rat fleas,' I said, as cheerily as I could. And I heard his mask move, and I felt his eyes on me as I carried on down the road; but I did not turn my head, for looking back is over for me now: and also, I had no wish to see his face.

Into the Nowhere

A cold poisonous wind blew across the abandoned wasteland. Some loose gravel, leached of colour, rattled across the barren ground. Above, an ever-moving, angry sky with roiling clouds fretted across the empty landscape.

Or not quite empty. Bleached by the wind, rubbed dry by the sand and stone, skeletons littered the earth as far as the eye could see, a jumble of femurs, knobbly spines, toes. A hank of colourless hair, here and there; a glint of something on the ground that might once have meant something to someone; and the skulls, everywhere, endless, all laughing the rictus of death under the grey and purple sky.

The little piece of gravel had stopped bouncing down the hill of scree, but after a long moment of silence, a tapping noise occurred. Then silence, then another one. At first it was simply a tap-tap-tap. Then it was joined by a low rattle, here and there. Almost indistinguishable from the little stones being tossed by the wind. Almost.

The bones were on the move again.

'Where are we?' said Clara, squinting at the screen.

There was a long silence. This was unusual. Clara looked around the console room.

'We appear to be in the TARDIS but the Doctor isn't talking,' said Clara to herself. 'This extraordinarily rare phenomenon is believed by some observers to be the result of his gob being immersed in a black hole... actually what are you doing? Have you got addicted to *Home and Away* again? Are you hungry? I have issues with people who never get hungry.'

The Doctor didn't even lift his head.

Clara jumped round the other side of the red-flashing console to where the Doctor was craning his neck at a large screen. On it, and replicated on the other monitor, was a sight far from unusual: a planet, orbiting a dull sun.

'Where are we?' she asked again.

At this the Doctor let out a sigh.

'What is *wrong* with you?' said Clara. 'Are you missing that dog thing again? You talk about that dog thing a lot.'

'Yes,' said the Doctor finally. 'But that's not it.' He stabbed a long finger at the planet on the screen. 'I don't like it,' he said crossly.

'It looks harmless,' said Clara. Storm patterns whorled around its surface.

'I'm sure it is,' said the Doctor. 'But still. I don't like it. Let's go somewhere else.' He started tinkering with a large lever.

'Hang on,' said Clara, a smile playing on her lips. 'Where is it? I mean, what's it called?'

The Doctor carried on tinkering.

'Ha! You don't know! That's why you're cross. You actually don't know something. Are we lost?'

'No! Absolutely not. Anyway, we never get lost. We occasionally. . . get fruitfully diverted.'

He patted the TARDIS fondly with his hand.

'Good' said Clara, putting her hand over his to stop him moving the dial. 'So, just tell me what this planet's called then we can get on our way.'

'Um. . . it's called. . . it's called. . .' The Doctor cast around the room for inspiration. 'It's called Hatstandia,' he said, then screwed up his face at the choice.

'Hatstandia?' said Clara. She pushed a button, which lit up red and glowered at her. 'Hush,' she said. 'I'm just checking.' She looked up. 'The TARDIS doesn't think it's called Hatstandia.' She stood back and folded her arms. 'Do *neither* of you know what it's called? *Now* it's getting interesting.'

'It's not on *any* maps,' said the Doctor crossly. 'It's not referenced anywhere. It's not in any of the literature.'

He threw a hand-sized item covered in buttons with a 'D' and a 'P' just visible on the cover across the control room, then checked to make sure it had had a safe landing.

'Normally if I don't recognise a planet then the TARDIS knows, or something knows, or I can find out somewhere,' he said, rubbing the back of his hair. 'This one, though. . . It's just nowhere. *Nowhere.*'

'Maybe it's just too dull to bother giving it a name,' said Clara.

'They named Clom,' said the Doctor. 'No, it would have a name. Or at the very least, it would still have coordinates and references. But this... It's like it's just appeared from nothing.'

'Oh, a *mysterious* planet,' said Clara. 'Well in that case we'd better leave it alone, don't you think? Just head off and never think about it again. Yup that will be best...'

They had already landed.

'Ugh! I hate this planet, it's rubbish. Look at all these rocks! Rubbish!' The Doctor hurled a stone far away into a crater. It bounced then skidded to a halt. There was a rattling noise.

'Not Gallifrey, then?'

The Doctor silenced her with a look.

Clara cast her eyes around to quickly change the subject. 'Did you hear something?' she said.

'No. Nothing.'

'Stop grumping,' said Clara, pulling her red cloak around her. She still felt the novelty of stepping out onto the ground of a completely different world. She looked up in the sky. There was a mouldy-looking burnt-orange old sun which gave out an ominously low sickly light. 'It's like travelling the universe with Alan Sugar. Anyway, I think you're being world-ist. Somebody must love this place; it's their home. You know, like Croydon.'

The Doctor gave her a look. 'Don't be daft, Croydon's got a tram museum. Croydon is *ace. Where's your tram museum, planet?*'

'What's that smell?' Clara asked, looking round in vain for any kind of interesting thing to fixate on.

The Doctor took a deep sniff. 'It's 78.09 per cent nitrogen, 20.95 per cent oxygen, 0.039 per cent carbon dioxide, 0.871 per cent argon, and 0.05 per cent sulphur, hence the *rotten eggy smell*, planet.'

'All right,' said Clara. 'OK, you win, let's go.' She turned back to the TARDIS

'Well I can't, can I?' said the Doctor sulkily, hurling another pebble into the middle distance. Once again, Clara thought she heard it rattle for longer that it ought to have done. 'Planet with its own atmosphere, not on any star charts, not recorded, not in the TARDIS data banks. Well, that's not right, is it?'

'You don't have to find out. You're not the policeman of the universe,' said Clara. 'No, wait, that's exactly what you are, isn't it? You've got the box and everything.'

The skeleton quivered as it lay on the ground; in order now, the bones having managed, slowly, to assemble themselves in the correct shape. Now it looked more like a body correctly laid out for burial. For a moment under the congealing sky all was still. Then slowly, carefully, a toe bone began to flex.

The Doctor strode forward. 'So now we just have to walk about until we find something. I'm hoping for an engraved plaque that says, "Oh, sorry, this is Planet Anthony, we forgot to mention it to anyone, not to worry, we peacefully ceased reproducing six billion years ago and it was all fine, have a nice day."'

'Planet *Anthony*?'

The Doctor sniffed, but said nothing.

'Well,' said Clara, setting off determinedly for the horizon. She mounted a small rocky bank. 'Maybe we could just say it's a pleasant constitutional.'

'Why are you going that way? I think we could do with a bit of colour. Can I wear my fez?'

'No,' said Clara, desperately trying not to lose her patience with him. 'And we can go the other way if you aaaaaaaah. . .'

The Doctor charged up the bank, then, carefully, back again, hopping as he felt his boots sink immediately. 'Argh, quicksand!' he shouted, throwing himself on the ground. 'Clara! Clara! Get out! We've landed in quicksand!'

But he was too late. Clara was already stuck in: hemmed in by a whirlpool of sand that was swirling round like water in a sink, sucking her down. The more she struggled, the more it was pulling her under. Her large dark eyes were full of terror.

'*Doctor!*'

'Try not to panic!'

'The sand is *eating me*! So, you know – *panic!*'

The sand was closing in on Clara. She could barely see the Doctor over the top of the ridge. Her body and chest felt entirely constrained, pushed in; her ribs couldn't move to breathe against the sheer weight of all the earth. She couldn't bear the thought of the sand reaching her mouth, but the more she tried to get her head free, the more it sucked her down, the sand whirling round and round her, the scent of old dust in her throat and in her nose, choking her. She pushed her head back as the sand reached her ears, the feeling revolting, the noise a roar: one hand now had been pushed back and was trapped behind her, wrenching and immobile.

Then the sand was in her mouth. One grain, then more, dry, dusty, choking.

'*No!*' she screamed, her throat raw, clenching and spitting at the muck. 'Doc—'

But then she was forced to close her mouth.

The Doctor was cursing his slow progress crawling over the side of the dune, tugging off the front buttons of his braces.

'This would probably have worked better with the fez!' he shouted, tying one end of the braces to a dead root that protruded from the dry earth, kept the other on, and dived in towards the sand, headfirst, reaching down. He forced himself down into the earth, groping downwards until he felt a hand, and quickly tied the final side of the braces to it, then forced himself upwards through pure will up against the cascading whirlwind of sand that was still pouring down like a huge draining sink.

Then he buttressed himself against the slope and began the agonising feat of dragging her out, as the elastic stretched and stretched and the Doctor feared it would not hold, as he pulled with all his might, shouting out with the exertion, as finally, slowly, emerged Clara, coughing and choking and covered in fine pale chalky sand. Once her arms were free, she could help herself and moved upwards more quickly.

They both scrambled up the bank, dusting themselves down.

'That was *disgusting*,' said Clara, finally, spitting sand out of her mouth.

'Yes, and—'

'Stop going on about a fez not being elastic,' said Clara, wiping out her mouth with her red cloak, thoroughly shaken up.

They turned round to look back the way they had come. Now, the quicksand seemed obvious – the entire landscape practically undulated all the way back to the TARDIS. The dark and light patches of sand and rubble now appeared ominous in the dull and purple tinged light, the TARDIS listing slightly to one side.

To their left were great mountain peaks, grey and forbidding. To their right, stretching out far, was a thick wood.

'Can you summon the TARDIS to come and get us?'

The Doctor rolled his eyes. 'Yes, Clara, and I've been keeping that from you all this time.' He looked at the TARDIS regretfully. 'She's not a dog.'

'Again with the dog,' said Clara, poking the last bits of sand out of the corners of her eyes.

The Doctor looked around the landscape suddenly.

'What are you looking for?'

'Nothing. Um. Discarded ladder?'

'Oh yes, it's just over there by the handy pile of rope,' said Clara. She too took in their surroundings.

They looked again at the dead and wintry-looking forest of bare trees, their crooked gnarled branches reaching towards the miserable sky at an angle, as if in supplication. They seemed to curve on for ever.

'Shall we try the trees?' said Clara. 'Maybe find a long way round?'

The Doctor was looking the other way, at the mountainous horizon. 'Hmmm…'

They both heard it this time.

A low, distinct rattle sounded, just audible above the howling wind. The Doctor spun around again, confirming the direction of the noise. 'Spooky woods?' he asked Clara.

'Definitely,' said Clara. 'We can climb the desolate mountains as a treat afterwards.'

They inched their way carefully along the stone ledge towards the trees. Despite her cloak, Clara was cold, and the sky threatened rain. Noise was travelling strangely and she was still shaken up by the awful feeling of being nearly buried alive. Of course, there was absolutely no way she was going to admit that to the tall figure cheerfully striding on ahead, his bad mood quite forgotten now there was a mystery to solve, looking for all the world as if he was having a Sunday stroll in the park.

'Hullloo!' he shouted as they approached the woods. 'Anyone here, rattling about? Rattling about, that's a joke, you see? It will disarm and intrigue them.'

He took out his sonic screwdriver and lit it up to give it a steady glow, but in fact, as the day had grown darker, this served rather to bring the immediate ground into sharp relief, whilst plunging everything else into shadow. Clara liked it distinctly less. The trees stretched out their gnarled empty branches likes arthritic arms. There wasn't a leaf or a speck of green to be seen on them anywhere, they were blasted black.

'Maybe it was just the wind whistling through the trees,' she said hopefully.

The rattling continued. It sounded nothing like trees. The Doctor shone his light on the ground ahead of them, and they both stopped, and gasped.

'That wasn't there before,' blurted out Clara.

55

'Maybe we've got a little confused,' said the Doctor, looking round. The trees on all sides looked exactly the same. It was much darker in the forest than he'd anticipated. But down on the ground, clear as day, there was a spelled out message in ash, like the remains of a bonfire, resting on the blackened twigs.

'K-N-O-W.'

Immediately Clara whipped her head round, but couldn't see anything.

'Well, now we're getting somewhere,' said the Doctor cheerily. 'Come and say hello. What should we know?'

Suddenly the two end letters were blown away by the wind, leaving behind only the N and the O.

Clara suddenly felt rather nervous. 'I'm not sure I want them to come and find us,' she said. 'What are they?'

'Dunno!' said the Doctor, marching on.

Clara bit her lip. She would have liked to have taken his hand, or even just held on to his coat. Sometimes his belief that everyone was as fearless as himself was encouraging and inspiring. Sometimes... it wasn't. She glanced behind her. Already, the ash message on the ground had been blown away by the noisy, ever-swirling wind.

They seemed to be getting deeper and deeper into a forest that had seemed little more than a thicket when they'd approached. But the normal sounds of a forest – birdsong, squirrels scampering – were all absent. It was like nothing lived there at all.

But they knew that something did.

'So, this is peculiar,' said the Doctor, shaking his sonic screwdriver.

'What's up?'

'Well, I've been heading directly for the TARDIS – I have a perfect sense of direction.'

Clara gave him a Hard Stare, but the Doctor didn't notice.

'We really ought to be there by now.'

'What do you mean?'

'I'm not sure,' he said. 'Unless there's something odd about the dimensions of this place... It's almost like the lost planet wants us to be lost too. But why?'

Suddenly, something caught the corner of Clara's eye and she started a little; she couldn't help it. It was just the faintest brush of something vanishing at speed through the trees; a white flash she wasn't even sure she had seen. But left behind, right there it was outlined on the ground; another message.

'NO.'

They looked at it for a moment.

'What do you reckon?' said Clara. 'Warning us off a delicious gingerbread house?'

'I think the trees are getting thicker,' said the Doctor. 'Like the forest is trying to keep us out.'

Clara glanced around. He was right. 'Do you mean... are those trees closer together than they were before?' she said, her heart starting to pound in her chest.

The Doctor looked behind them. 'Now you mention it.'

As he said this, behind them the way they had come appeared to have closed over completely in a tangle of dead, wiry branches, blocking their retreat. It was getting darker and darker overhead.

'Uh-oh,' said Clara.

'"The best way out is always through,"' mused the Doctor. 'Do you know, I think this calls for a bit of the old you-know-what.'

Clara knew they were not imagining it, even though as they ran it felt like a panicky dream from which she could not awaken.

The trees were moving in the wind as if they were alive; they were twisting towards her; stretching out ancient gnarled fingers, trapping in her hair, clutching at her dress, ripping her clothes. Her heart was pounding in her ears and she could feel her own breath tearing at her throat.

Twisted vines shot up from nowhere, branches appeared, separating them, until she could no longer see the Doctor, could see nothing except the next gap or the next hole in the twisted, splitting wall of nightmarish rotting branches and black encroaching trees.

She was completely lost now, her mind blind to anything but the call to flee. She could not tell one way from another, had no sense of where the TARDIS or even the Doctor might be or might once have been, as the forest swelled to fill her entire world. Half of her red cloak was gone, torn off on a persistent branch, her hair had escaped its bun and had fallen all round her face, and still she ran on.

At last she saw a light glinting ahead through the black thicket of trees and the heavy grey of the sky, and she pounded on towards it.

'Clara!'

The Doctor was calling her, but she couldn't hear, as the blood crashed around her head and all she could feel was branches pulling at her. He snatched up her red cloak.

'Clara!'

Still he could not get through, even as he started to run towards her, confounded as to how she could be charging so hard towards it.

'*Clara!*' He was running at full pelt now, astonished she had not seen the danger, incredulous she had not stopped. '*Clara!!!!!!*'

At the last instant, she heard him. Heard something. She turned her head – and immediately a branch shot out and knocked her to the ground. The last thing she saw was the light opening up in front of her; a huge pit of fire that was consuming the trees and heading towards them.

How had she not smelt the burning, felt the force of the licking flames, the indescribable heat? He scooped her up and glanced around the burning wood, searching for an exit, any way out. The flames were coming faster and faster. Behind him, the woods had closed up against him; the trees were now a solid wall of wood, completely entwined with each other, already starting to smoulder. To the side of the clearing too, the trees were too thick.

'Alors,' said the Doctor to himself, then, looking down at Clara's unconscious face in her arms, took a deep breath, then covered her entirely with the red cloak and picked her up. He turned up the collar of his jacket and quickly smoothed down his eyebrows. Then he blinked rapidly twice, took a deep breath, put the

collar up over his mouth, and ran straight into the wall
of flame.

He had taken a long run-up and stretched out his
legs as far as they could go to get as much clearance on
the other side as possible, and he made it. He felt his hair
scorch, the smell of burning in his nostrils as he took a
huge leap through the raging walls of flame, one which
caught the trail of Clara's cloak. He rolled her briskly
on the ground to beat out the flames, muttering briefly,
'Please don't wake up right now' as he did so, then
blinked the smoke out of his eyes and looked ahead.

'Gah,' he said, as his eyes took in the horrifying vista.
'Naughty Planet Anthony, why do I think you're doing
this on purpose?'

They were perched right on the edge of an impossibly
vertiginous cliff, over which he had very nearly rolled
them both, scree scattering below. The fire was still
raging right behind them, cutting off their escape route,
but the precipice was perilously high.

The Doctor went to peer over the top of it. It was
so steep he had to bend his head out quite far to see
the bottom of the vast mountain. Ugly grey tufts
were floating beneath them; they were higher than
the clouds.

At the bottom of the cliff, at least a kilometre
down, was something that at first the Doctor took for
a white, foaming river. As he looked closer, however,
he saw that it was something – no, many things
– moving. Alive. A squirming, writing mass of. . .
something. He couldn't tell what. Beasts of some
kind. They looked like impossibly large churning
maggots. He arched an eyebrow and sat back, no

longer able to pretend to himself that their bad luck was coincidental.

Behind him, Clara was sitting up, rubbing her head and trying to remember where she was. When she saw the Doctor, her face broke into a relieved smile.

'Oh, thank goodness,' she said, sitting up carefully, clutching her head. 'We're safe!'

'Ye-es. . .' said the Doctor. He frowned and looked over to the far side of the abyss. 'I wish I'd packed a flask.'

He looked up to the other side. Slowly, out of the chilly mists on the far side, a figure was approaching, dressed in a faded cloak with the hood up. It moved slowly and seemed both human and not at the same time. The Doctor moved nearer to watch the figure approach, as Clara gradually pulled herself to her feet, looking in fear at the fire still blazing behind them.

'You're too close to the edge,' she shouted.

'My favourite spot,' said the Doctor, still concentrating hard on the opposite cliff side.

The figure stood there, and its cloak hood fell back. It was not a person; or rather, it was no longer a person. It was an empty, gleaming skull, picked and polished white, and the odd, human-esque figure beneath the cloak was also skeletal; it was made entirely of bone. A walking skeleton.

The Doctor blinked rapidly. 'Well, that's unusual,' he said.

'*Unusual*?' said Clara, beside him. 'He's not a new chair.'

The Doctor ignored her, lifted up his hands to his mouth and hollered across the abyss. 'Hallo there! Nice to meet you!'

'Politeness,' muttered Clara to herself. 'Always important to politely introduce yourself to a *hideous death skeleton*.'

'Who are you? I'm the Doctor, this is—'

'Don't tell him my name!' said Clara. 'What if it's Death, come to claim us? I don't want him to find me.'

'Nah,' said the Doctor. 'Death rides a skeletal horse, too. I'm kidding, I'm kidding.'

The skeleton stared at them, then lifted its bony left arm, one long white finger raw and gleaming, as if pointing at them.

It then raised its right hand, which contained a long, slim, very sharp knife. Then it leant its hand over the side of the canyon, above a grassy outcrop, and started, with delicate movements, to shave off tiny fractions of the bone. They fell onto the gorse, and formed immediately into letters. Clara winced.

'KNOW,' the letters spelled in white powder, the 'K' and the 'W' fading away with the wind, just as they'd seen inside the forest.

'Well, yes, we got that one,' said the Doctor. 'I will say, this isn't the most welcoming spot we've ever visited.'

'That's disgusting,' said Clara.

The Doctor looked along the cliff edge. To the left there was another clump of trees past were the fire had burned out, thick and dense with black, but Clara thought she saw something glinting in the twisted branches; something that made her instinctively flinch.

Ahead was the canyon, and the scorched wasteland ahead showed the skeletal figure silhouetted in the gathering dust. The other side was not far, but it was too far to jump, and the precipice was horribly steep.

'I want to go and chat to him,' said the Doctor decisively. 'I wish I could reach him on the telebone. Ha! Telebone!'

Clara gave him a look.

'Excuse me!' hollered the Doctor. 'Is there a bridge? Can we come and talk to you?'

The figure stayed completely still, then slowly turned and began walking away.

'After him,' said the Doctor. 'There has to be a way across somewhere.'

But to their right, there was nothing as the cliff sheered off. And to the left, they plunged head first into the newest copse of trees.

Clara caught sight of it again out of the corner of her eye. Just a sense of movement, a flicker she could not pin down, but that sent a cold-fingered shudder down her spine that wasn't just the chilling wind. She slowed a little.

'Hmm,' said the Doctor. 'There must be a bridge somewhere round here. Impossible physical skeletons can't fly.'

The next time the Doctor saw it too.

'Hey! There's something up those trees.'

'I was considering pretending I hadn't seen it,' said Clara, 'in the hope that it might go away.' She wrapped her arms in the remnant of the red cloak, and briefly considered putting it over her head, so she wouldn't have to look.

As they approached, Clara saw the movement more clearly: an intense, muscular writhing; brown and copper scales glinting in the half-light, great heavy coils hanging down from branches.

'Well, aren't you beautiful,' breathed the Doctor. 'How on earth do you survive here? What do you eat?'

'*Doctor!*' screamed Clara.

The huge head of the enormous snake shot out with extraordinary speed, its massive jaws impossibly wide, a loud hiss of furious expelled air. The Doctor lurched back, startled, as the hideous creature missed him by inches, then retreated its massive body in preparation for a second strike, its ghastly pink maw wide apart.

'Us!' said Clara. 'It's going to eat *us*!'

'Extraordinary animal,' whispered the Doctor in awe. 'Pure predator.'

They were backing away when Clara heard another malevolent hiss from right behind her. She jumped. The Doctor took out his sonic screwdriver and held it up.

'Now,' he said calmly to Clara. 'The thing about a really big snake is, much as I would hate to hurt her, it pays to be prepared, just in case you ever have to cut your way out from the inside.'

The huge head veered at them again; Clara could see more writhing in the trees around them and found herself backing towards the edge of the cliff. A rattle of scree tumbled down as her foot slipped back on the very edge. Clara was trying to do the odds in her panicking brain; would she rather tumble down a cliff side or be eaten by a snake?

The huge brown snake was rearing again, preparing for another strike, the branch was right above their head, and there was no time left now to think at all. She grasped the Doctor's coat, faintly, for comfort. But he was busy, darting right and left, the snake following, weaving its massive body, its slitted eyes fixed on the Doctor's.

'Can it hypnotise you?' said Clara, her breath stopping in her throat.

'It can try!' said the Doctor gleefully. 'But fortunately my Parseltongue is excellent... I'll talk her out of it somehow – Aha!'

He fumbled with a setting on his sonic screwdriver, which started to vibrate in his hand, glowing a faint blue and, to Clara's utter astonishment, bravely stuck his hand straight up in the air in front of the snake's face and beamed the light into its eyes.

She waited for the creature to devour him fingers first, but instead, the snake hesitated then caught the light with its gaze. Gently, the Doctor waggled his screwdriver from side to side, and the snake followed, weaving its massive head from side to side.

'Ha!' said the Doctor. 'And also: phew!'

He slowed his arm motion down and gently moved his hand from side to side as if conducting an orchestra. As he did so, the snake slowly closed its jaws and started to undulate itself, huge shivers passing along its elongated body. Gradually, the coils relaxed and the huge long tail unfurled and drooped to the ground.

'OK,' said the Doctor in a low voice, not taking his eyes off the snake, or slowing the relentless hypnotic movement of his hand. 'We are almost certainly only going to get one shot at this.'

Clara moved quietly too. The snake's head followed the Doctor's hand, as he carefully inched around.

'Now,' he said, quickly indicating with his eyes and speaking very quietly.

'You are joking,' said Clara.

'No,' said the Doctor, eyes on the snake. 'Because normally my jokes are brilliant, and this, right now, would be a terrible joke, don't you think? I think I would lose my reputation for my wonderful jokes. You know, like that one about the telebone?'

'Yes, that one,' said Clara. She looked ahead at what he was indicating. It was the ravine, the cliff's edge. And, hanging off the tree, the long, long tale of a snake, looking very like a rope.

'Won't we just pull down the snake?'

The Doctor shook his head. 'No, her instincts will make her grip on. Might hurt a bit, pulling her tail, but that can't be helped.' The hissing from the other trees grew louder and the Doctor frowned. 'They're asking what she's doing. They're getting suspicious. So, are you ready?'

'Am I ready to swing over a precipice by snake's tail?' said Clara.

'Yeah! I know, new thing!' said the Doctor gleefully.

He speeded his hand up momentarily, as the snake looked as if it was settling down to sleep, its tail waving lazily in the wind. They backed away as far as they could without coming up against one of the snake's friends in the other trees.

'1 . . . 2 . . . 3 . . .'

Then they both ran and jumped and swung, the forward momentum carrying them forward straight out over the cliff's edge. A fierce wind blew right through them. Clara clung with one arm to the Doctor, one to the surprisingly warm, smooth body of the beast. She felt it tighten from the top, obviously clinging on to the tree and was only conscious of the Doctor shouting '*Jump!*' before the snake's tail slithered out of their grasp and she felt herself thudding into the other side of the cliff, bumping her head and getting a mouthful of rock and dirt, taking the skin off her hands and knees, grazing her cheeks but clinging on; clinging on for dear life. She risked a look down then regretted it instantly, and instead concentrated on hauling herself up and over the ledge, grabbing the strong arm that reached down for her.

'You know, my old mate Tarzan used to do this all the time,' confided the Doctor. 'He said it was vines, but we knew the truth.'

Clara wasn't listening. She had stopped short, staring straight ahead. Then she let out a sharp cry of surprise and relief.

'*Clara!*'

But Clara had already torn away, dashed over to the sight she was so desperate to see: the TARDIS was there, the familiar blue box that was, impossibly, standing completely by itself on the flat rocky plain this side of the abyss. Clara ran with her arms outstretched as if to embrace it.

The Doctor watched, sadly, as she reached the mirage TARDIS, as she carried on, ran through it, the fake blue light shimmering, rendering the box nothing more than the illusion it was.

He had known straight away, of course. He could recognise his own TARDIS, and he knew this wasn't it; rather a foul trick. But Clara's face, as she turned, put her hand through the blue light image, waved it around, then sank to the ground, was completely desolate and wretched.

'What?' said the Doctor, wandering over. He marched right through the fake TARDIS. 'You've gone a really weird white colour.'

'Because obviously I am having a *really bad day*!' Clara stood up, launched herself at him and buried her face in his jacket.

'You're all wobbly!'

'I'm *shaking*.'

'Really? Teeth and everything? Let me see your teeth, that's my favourite bit.'

She showed him her chattering mouth.

'Ha. Excellent. You can nibble your way out of trouble.'

Tenderly, he took out his handkerchief and wiped away the tiny beads of blood from her forehead. Night was falling fast on the vast inhospitable landscape and it was terribly cold.

'I thought it was quite fun, me rescuing you for a change.'

'Well, how about I don't want anyone to be rescuing anyone?' said Clara, drawing back.

She knew she sounded sulky, but she couldn't help herself. Sometimes, when travelling with the Doctor, she felt. . . it was hard to explain, even to herself. It was if her true feelings were buried under so many layers that sometimes it was hard to tell what was real and what was just a dream.

Clara pouted. Then she pouted again, because if you didn't make it really clear to the Doctor that you were sulking, he was simply incapable of noticing. Even now he was scanning the horizon, plotting their next course.

He turned round and finally clocked her face.

'Ah. Clara. You're... you're not happy are you?'

'Apart from the quicksand and the moving forest and the fire and the fact that I have *snake* on me? No. I'm great!'

There was a very long pause between them. Then finally the Doctor sighed. 'Look. The thing is...'

She could tell he was trying to be tactful, which she appreciated, because she knew he absolutely did not have the knack.

'The thing is, most people who come travelling with me...'

A faint look of weariness passed over his face.

'Most people... they love it. They love it. And I get to experience a universe I know too well; I get to experience it through their eyes, through fresh eyes. And I need that.'

Clara nodded, feeling suddenly rather tearful.

'What I mean is, I can't promise everything will be all right, I can only promise that it will be interesting. And fun, and wonderful and cool and amazing. But you have to open your eyes.'

'To the beauty of snakes,' said Clara quietly.

'The beauty of snakes,' said the Doctor, nodding his head vehemently. 'Exactly.'

Clara nodded too. *But I'm not*, she suddenly found herself thinking, a voice from deep within her. *I'm not one of your other innocent chums, your buddies you go yomping around with, who 'love' adventures, because they have never learned the cost.*

She wondered what she meant. Her head hurt suddenly.

The odd voice inside her piped up again: *I have known it*, it said. *As deep in my bones as the skeletons who walk here: what it feels like and what it costs me, and I do not think that snakes are beautiful. Did they say they would, all those others? Did they say they would die for you and suffer for you and live life as an open wound for you? And did they? Or do they go to sleep at night safe and warm in their beds?*

But as quickly as the thought crossed her mind, it rippled away, like shaking off the dust of a fast-fading morning dream. Clara shook her head, which cleared instantly, and blinked away the tears that had somehow started to form in her eyes. 'You're right,' she said, pulling herself together. 'Of course you're right. I'm fine. Again?' she said, indicating left, the purple mountains, the weakening, barely noticeable sun going down, rattlings coming right and left, night coming in on this horrible planet filled with monsters.

The Doctor gave her a wink. 'Once more unto the breach, dear friend?'

'Once more,' said Clara, a sweet smile spreading across her face, as she once again suppressed and forgot the tumult within.

'Who would build this torture garden?'

For that, as the Doctor looked around, was clearly what it was. In the distance he could see lines and lines of barbed wire – landmines? It made no sense. They were being watched, but why the multitude of ways to kill or horribly injure yourself? He and Clara only just skirted a massive mantrap, set up outside a small cave, obviously there to trap the sleepy and unwary.

The chill wind blew right through them as they walked on without speaking, Clara gathering the cloak around herself, her face set against the weather. Finally, across the landscape, the figure they were both following and dreading to see revealed itself; first a dot on the horizon, moving slowly, looking, from this distance, once more like a man. It was only as they grew closer that the hideous skeletal form revealed itself, the pale white bone glinting in the watery moonlight of the two pale moons.

'Ahoy!' shouted the Doctor. 'Where are you off to, matey?'

The skeleton wore its rictus grin, but the slumped posture and weary walk made it seem defeated. Clara, oddly, had the very strong impression that it was sad.

'Where are you going?' said the Doctor.

The skeleton held up his scalpel again, and Clara looked away. The shavings of bone formed on the ground.

'*Le Roi des Os,*' it spelled on the ground. Everything except the 'O's quickly scattered.

'Le Roi des Os,' said the Doctor. 'Oh, you're French.'

Clara stared at it too. 'The King of Bones,' she read.

'You belong to the King of Bones?' said the Doctor.

The skeleton's sightless eyes were still pointing in the direction of the far horizon as it nodded.

'Who is he?' The Doctor circled him, looking closely. The rattling head followed them wherever they went, the scalpel held high. Then he saw it. 'Cor!' he said suddenly. 'They did a right job on you. Come and have a look, Clara.'

'Must I?'

'Look!' The Doctor pointed out near invisible, very thin pale wires that connected the bones to each other.

'Carnutium filaments. Practically undetectable, but send signals at nearly the speed of light. You, my friend are the most astonishing thing, look at you.'

The skeleton turned its head very slowly to look at the Doctor, who was standing behind him.

'Human bones held with electro-stimulating filaments. You are the weirdest robots ever. Why can't you talk?'

The skeleton held up the scalpel again.

'No,' said the Doctor. 'Don't do that. Does it hurt you?'

The skeleton did not move.

'He doesn't want you to talk, does he? The King of Bones? He wants you to do his bidding silently. Is that it?'

'Is there a person in there?' said Clara in horror.

'Y-o-u-a-r-e-n-o-t-a-f-r-a-i-d-o-f-u-s,' spelled the skeleton slowly on the ground.

The Doctor looked at him aghast. 'How could I be?' he said, his voice breaking with pity.

The skeleton stood still for a moment.

'C-O-M-E,' he spelled on the ground, and he trudged on.

They followed a strange path, sometimes veering wildly to the right, sometimes doubling back. The Doctor inferred, correctly, that the skeleton was avoiding deadly traps in the dark of the night, and was grateful, but worried about where they were being led. If the King of Bones did not want them dead, what did he want with them?

All the way he talked non-stop to the skeleton, telling him silly French jokes and singing songs and trying to get a reaction from him that wasn't a scalpel.

'Does he,' he said finally, 'does he make you do things you don't want to do, the Roi des Os? Does he make you? Ooh, Boney! Like that other French bloke, Napoleon. Now, as you know, I like everyone...'

The figure suddenly stopped, and the great empty pits of eyeholes trained themselves on the Doctor. There was an uncharacteristically long pause.

'Um, OK, carry on,' said the Doctor finally, clearing his throat.

Just as he did so, a crackle of light raced up the filaments that bound the skeleton together and it jerked backwards as if shocked. Then it turned to face forwards again, and the party continued.

Although later Clara realised it was only a few hours, that cold and exhausting journey, across the ruined world, dotted here and there with blast craters and the occasional howl, seemed to her to take forever.

Finally, over the crest of a crumbled hill, they saw it, eerily gleaming by the light of the pallid moons. The only building on, it seemed, the entire world. It was built of white marble, Clara thought at first, and was beautiful in the manner of the Taj Mahal but, as she grew closer, swallowing madly, she realised that it was in fact constructed of bones: thousands, hundreds of thousands of bones, like planking on the huge structure. It had rows of windows, the knobbly extrusions of femurs all lined up neatly; smaller crossed bones making decorative patterns around the arched doorframes.

Clara felt the breath catch in her throat. The awful beauty of the palace was undeniable, built though it was on a slaughterhouse. Silent skeletons stood in rows as sentries; there were hundreds of them. She gasped and nudged the Doctor. Over to the side, standing like the others, its head ridiculously large in comparison to its body, standing with the rest, was the unmistakeable skeleton of a child.

The Doctor blinked twice, rapidly, and marched up to the front door. 'Thank you,' he said to the skeleton who had led them there so silently. '*Courage, mon brave.*'

And he looked at the doorknocker, comprised of finger bones, and left it behind, rapping instead with his knuckles, but there was no reply.

He pushed at the door and it opened, slowly. Inside, it was dark, musty smelling, oppressively warm. There was not a sound to be heard.

Clara could hear the blood pounding in her head, the rhythm of her own heart.

The Doctor turned to her with a sudden wink. 'I don't know about you,' he said, quietly. 'But I haven't met many goodies who live in houses like this.'

The first room they entered was covered in weaponry: scores of swords, guns, lasers and axes hanging on the bone walls. Next they passed a stairwell, leading downwards into the dark. Clara thought she could see a faint light coming from the basement, but the Doctor stalked on.

'Watch out for booby traps,' he said, which wasn't helpful as the house was dusty and gloomy, and Clara fully expected the floor to give way with every step.

Moving further in – still they had seen no one, heard nothing – the walls were hung with red woven tapestries that deadened the sound of their footsteps. Dust lay thickly everywhere, under an oppressive layer of heat, and the air was heavy with the scent of decay.

Suddenly Clara stopped. 'Listen,' she said.

They did. It sounded like... it was... music. Definitely music. Strange and complex, and played on instruments that Clara didn't recognise, but it was music. They headed for one of the many doors in that direction, getting closer to it. One of the arched doors was swinging slightly open. That was the room where the music was playing loudly. It was rather beautiful.

The Doctor cleared his throat and knocked loudly on the side of the archway. 'Hullo?'

Again, there was no response, and they made their way slowly forwards.

It was so dark in the room it took a couple of seconds for Clara's eyes to focus; she could barely make out what she was looking at. It couldn't possibly, she thought at first, be a living person, a real one. But, as her eyes adjusted, she realised it was: in fact, it was a young man, but he was also incredibly, grotesquely fat, so fat he could barely move.

His skin was pitted with huge red spots, angry and infected-looking. He wore glasses, which were stretched out either side of his head, and his unwieldy mass was perched on some kind of a cushion arrangement that moulded to his distorted limbs.

The man was wearing a huge, dirty shirt with a row of what looked like pens in the top pocket. Everywhere around him were plates of dirty and discarded food piled up; a large hookah, empty bottles, crumpled up paper, screens. It looked, Clara thought with some astonishment, like the world's messiest teenage bedroom, with the world's largest teenager. It smelled like it too. Rows of screens displaying different areas they had already been through lit up and flashed, and the man's fingers played rapidly over the tops of them, as if it were a fast action video game. There was also a large white-glowing console in his other hand.

Everyone held their breath for a beat.

'Oh yeah, hi,' came a breathy, nasal voice finally, faux casually. 'So, well done for getting this far, yeah? Most people don't.' He pulled a 'what can you do?' face, before picking something up off one of the dirty plates, sniffing it, then eating it and wiping his hands on the large undergarment he was wearing.

'*You're* the King of Bones?' said the Doctor.

The man raised his eyebrows. 'Wow, very good, you got them to talk to you.' His face turned stern. 'I told them not to do that. I stopped them talking, stopped them signing, stopped them writing in sand, and now this. Waste of good bone. Stupid robots.'

His eyes blinked behind the thick-lensed glasses. Clara had the very clear impression he didn't need them; that they were not his, but a trophy.

'Who are you? You guys seem a bit cool about the whole thing,' he said, sounding disappointed. 'Normally everyone is gibbering by the time they get here. Vomit, wet pants, the lot.'

Clara swallowed crossly. 'He's the Doctor and I'm Clara. We don't scare easily,' she said, in her strongest voice.

He just stared at them. 'He doesn't,' he said, not taking his eyes off Clara.

'I don't like your house,' said the Doctor.

'I don't like your jacket,' said the man. 'But I'm far too polite to mention it.'

'Did you build this place?'

'I did,' said the man. 'With blood, sweat, tears. And some bones.' He barked an awkward laugh at his own joke.

The Doctor squinted at him. 'But why? What reason?'

The man shrugged huge beefy shoulders and said the last thing the Doctor had expected to hear. 'It's my job, mate.'

Clara leaned forward. Sure enough, he had a faded, encrusted nametag clipped onto his shirt pocket. It looked completely incongruous in the hideous room. 'Etienne Boyce,' she read aloud.

The man smiled. His teeth were blackened and ghastly, his gums so pink they looked blood red. Clara could smell the decay from clear across the room.

'What kind of job is this?' said the Doctor, struggling to hold on to his temper.

The man blinked very rapidly. 'Security,' he said. 'I'm in computer security.' He indicated the bank of monitors surrounding him. 'Well, I was. Bit more of a freelance these days.'

Clara gasped 'This is a computer simulation?'

The man laughed. 'No! Please. I'm not some ruddy amateur.' He put his hands over his belly in satisfaction. 'Everything here is real. With a few modifications.'

'You've gone rogue?' said the Doctor.

'Best analyst in my division,' said Etienne proudly. 'Was just too good. Don't know how they thought they'd keep tabs on me.'

'Are you a hacker?' asked Clara timidly.

'The best. Hacked the Nestene Consciousness when I was 14. Resting Consciousness more like. Nestene Semi-consciousness, I call it.'

Again came the peculiar barking laugh of someone who didn't spend a lot of time conversing with other human beings. The man took another large bite of something he had found on a plate beside him and belched loudly.

The Doctor look around, nodding. 'So you're keeping this place secure?' he said. 'You were sent to hide this planet. And you did – even from the people who sent you?'

The man sighed. 'Well, yes. I am brilliant. But I still get the odd adventurer turning up. The odd person who won't take a telling. Plenty of crashes of course – that's a hazard of not turning up on navigational equipment. Still got to stop you all. That's my job. Was my job.'

'So, just to get this straight in my head,' said the Doctor, 'you're not here to protect us from the dangers of this planet.'

Etienne laughed again. It was a horrible barking sound. 'No, mate.'

'You made it this way.'

The man wiped his greasy fingers on a filthy napkin.

'It is unspeakable,' said the Doctor, 'what you have done to the people who landed here.'

'Come on, are you joking? Carnutium filament? It's brilliant! And it's not like I *kill* them. They die, and I just use the leftovers.'

'But there's a million things here that can kill you!' burst in Clara.

'Yes, because I have to protect the planet,' said Etienne, as if explaining things to a slow child.

'But those are people!' Clara was still horrified.

'*Were*,' said Etienne. He checked his console. 'Oooh, acid rainstorm coming up. You don't wanna be out in that. You know, I've got the Carnutium machine downstairs. Would be jumping the gun a bit, but it's totally painless, probably.' He looked at Clara. 'Or you can stay a bit, if you like.'

'But why?' said the Doctor, almost to himself. 'Who wanted a whole planet hidden? Who wanted something off the map so badly they would send a nutcase like you to do it? Why not just blow it up?'

Clara leant forward. The old photograph on the ID card was of a much slimmer, very young man – a teenager, really, all Adam's apple and awkwardness, the bare whisper of a moustache on his top lip, in a neat white shirt, looking for all the world completely and utterly normal.

Etienne shrugged. 'Job's a job, innit. Then they started complaining about my methods, so. . .' He blew on his fingers and opened them up.

'You disappeared for good,' said the Doctor.

'And I want to stay that way,' said Etienne. 'Guards, take them downstairs!' he screamed suddenly, in a startling contrast to his laidback speaking voice, and immediately four skeletons came to the door.

Once again, Clara flinched as the ghostly shapes emerged, their feet clacking on the floor. Then she saw the little one was with them, the child.

Overcome, Clara forgot everything: her fear, her exhaustion, her surroundings; forgot absolutely everything, except the many children over the years and centuries who had been in her care; some she remembered, some who were nothing more than dreams: the new and certain knowledge that these too had been people once, even if they were only robot-operated bones now; even if, whatever the Doctor thought, nothing of them remained except the hideous mechanisation of this man who animated the dead.

On pure instinct alone, she knelt down and opened her arms.

There was a moment's pause in the hideous, stinking, oppressive cavernous room built of the bones of the dead and the lost, the fat discontented king on his dead throne in his charnel house, ruling an empty wasteland.

Unsure it wasn't the last thing she'd ever do, she held her arms wide, shaking once more. And with a rattling and a clicking, its oversized pale white skull, the bones as smooth and cool as a snake's, breaking free of its programming, the skeleton child ran into her arms.

Clara knelt there waiting for a blow to fall, her eyes closed once again, but it did not. She glanced up. The Doctor and Etienne were both staring at her.

'That's new,' said Etienne, still chewing. 'Huh. Hey, insensate matter!' He held up the white shining console, menacingly. 'Seize her! Down below!'

There was a long pause. Then another skeleton, shorter than the other two, stepped towards Clara, foot bones rattling on the floor. Here it comes, thought Clara.

Instead, the skeleton moved towards her – then knelt down next to her, and took the smaller skeleton in its arms, cradling it like a baby.

'Aha!' shouted the Doctor in delight. 'Clara, you're amazing! Look at that. There is something left behind! Which makes *you* a monster,' he said, turning to Etienne.

'They can't feel a thing,' groused Etienne. 'Sometimes I have to readjust the mechanism, you know, bit of a shock just to keep 'em in position, that kind of a thing. But they're just. . . it's just bones I find lying about. Did the same thing with the trees, and they didn't mind.'

The Doctor looked at him, shaking his head, and turned to address the skeletons. 'You don't have to move for him, you know.'

'Oh yes they do,' said Etienne, sweat popping out on his vast forehead.

He pressed down a white button in the middle of the console, and instantly the crackle of white light pervaded the skeletons, causing them to stiffen and throw their heads back in what was clearly pain.

'No!' said the Doctor, whipping out his screwdriver and pressing another button, making both devices squeal with feedback. 'No, you don't.'

The remote exploded in Etienne's hand and he dropped it rapidly, swearing. He then looked up, his eyes full of fear, as he gazed at the wall of white in front of him.

The Doctor advanced. 'Tell me,' he said sternly. 'Tell me what it is you're protecting that's so special.'

Etienne gave them a twisted smile. 'Make me.'

'You're a child,' said the Doctor, dismayed. 'How old are you, anyway?'

The ruin of a man looked down. 'Dunno,' he said quietly, inching towards the remote control. 'But I am so good at my job.'

The Doctor scowled, grabbed the remote from the floor and stuck it in his top pocket. 'Stay there,' he said. 'Skeletons, can you watch him?'

One held up his finger.

'No, don't do that! Just nod!'

The largest of them nodded.

'Come on,' said the Doctor to Clara. 'Let's figure this out.'

Etienne cringed back a bit then sneered, grabbed one of his screen consoles and started typing feverishly on it.

The Doctor took Clara out into the corridor, and told her to stay where she was. Then he went down to the basement. When he returned, his face was grim, and Clara knew better than to ever ask him about it.

'Now,' he said. 'To business.'

They explored the entire palace, each room more shocking that the one before it. One contained endless boxes of pre-prepared food in cardboard boxes, with a huge hole carved out of it, dirty containers and utensils thrown and scattered about knee-deep, new ones grabbed at will. The smell was unholy. Another was filled with boxes and boxes of seeds, fruit, vegetables, flowers, fertilisers, geodesic domes and water filters, all of it untouched.

There was a room with a weather console, which as far as Clara could see didn't just tell you the weather; it created it.

One room had a huge loom, which had never been used and was clearly falling apart. There was a thrumming cold-storage facility that contained frozen specimens of animals and plants. In one vast workshop, cannibalised parts of spaceships had been put together – beautifully, intricately – into new, sinister-looking machines. One room was full of old spacesuits from different planets and ages; personal documents tossed in as if a huge trash can; hundreds, thousands of them.

One room had fresh linen, faded now and thick with dust: one had books, a huge library, everything one could ever need in any language, sitting in long, untouched rows except here and there, where one had been dragged out and thrown or despoiled or a batch had been burnt for whatever reason.

At this, the Doctor's mouth turned into a thin straight line and he turned abruptly and marched back into Etienne's stateroom. Etienne was typing furiously in the corner, his fleshy mouth pouting, grunting as he heaved himself up. Sweat was dripping from his forehead, and he was drinking something from a long container. The skeletons lined the far wall, blocking his exit. They appeared frozen.

'You could have built a paradise here,' said the Doctor furiously. 'You could have done anything and you have rendered this entire planet a blasted heath.'

Etienne suddenly started to laugh a wheezing laugh. His vast belly heaved and wobbled with the effort. 'A *paradise*?' he roared. 'Ha! The one thing they are here to prevent. A paradise. Oh, Doctor, my only job is to not long for paradise.'

The Doctor stared at him for a long time, his mind working furiously. 'Who sent you?'

Etienne shrugged. 'Can't remember. It was a lifetime ago. A different life. A lot of these.' He held up a bottle.

The Doctor strode forward and attempted to read the faded nametag on his filthy shirt.

Etienne laughed in his face. 'Now you're getting desperate,' he said, his breath foul. 'Doncha wanna know? Oh, I cut them loose. They were no use at all. But you really want what you came here to find? What my job – my *job* – is to keep hidden? You really want it?' Etienne stared into the Doctor's eyes for a long time. 'No way,' he said. 'I can see it. I can see it in your eyes. You've been here before. Ha! You *do* know where you are. Well, well.'

You would have had to have been studying the Doctor's face at very close quarters just then to see the tiny flash of understanding that passed across it. He immediately straightened up and backed away.

'Oh, there it is,' leered Etienne. 'You do know. Well then. Ha. No point in torturing you. You're there already. I thought we'd finally passed into myth. Well, well, well. There aren't many left like you these days.'

'There aren't,' growled the Doctor.

'Well, why don't I show the pretty one? That's why you've brought her back, right?'

'No!'

But Etienne had grabbed another device from the clutter around his chair, a tiny one this time, and pressed a button. Instantly there came the clanging and groaning of an ancient set of chains.

'Don't, Etienne,' said the Doctor, his tone quite different. 'We'll go. We'll turn around and we'll go. Right now.'

Clara shot round to look at him in amazement.

'Hang on, where's the conquering robot-freeing hero now?' said Etienne, looking amused. 'Where's the liberator of this planet, huh? Where's the person who's come to tell off naughty Etienne for his naughty behaviour?'

'Doctor?' said Clara, puzzled. The rattling noise continued.

'Leave!' the Doctor shouted at Clara. 'Get out! Get out of here!' He tried to grab the tiny button from Etienne, who raised his eyebrows and, laughing, hurled it in his mouth.

'Oh, for crying out loud,' said the Doctor, launching himself at Etienne and trying to pinch his nose. 'Clara, *go!*'

But it was too late. Slowly at first, a door in the wall of the house of bones had started to lower itself, drawbridge-style, into the open air. Clara expected of course to see into the dark, cold and storm-ridden night of the Nowhere planet.

Instead, a piercing shaft of glorious sunlight suddenly penetrated the mote-ridden fustiness of the shut-up scarlet room. A draft of fresh, clean, sweet air invaded the space. It was the kind of freshness you get on the first day after a long rainy spell, when it feels as if the earth has been washed clean. It was like waking up on a mountainside, or flying somewhere warm after a long winter.

They heard something else, too, for the first time: the silvering tones of birdsong, the type of spring morning

85

song that makes the heart clench. As the drawbridge drew down inch by inch, tiny wisps of cloud could be seen, floating across a Wedgewood blue sky; the golden light was soft and the sweet wind was scented with lotus flowers and apple. Beneath the birdsong, a fountain could be heard somewhere bubbling away merrily.

'Clara, ignore it. It's a force field. You can't go out there, it's a trap.'

'Oh no, there's no more traps left, mate,' giggled Etienne. His odd glasses had turned completely black, protecting his eyes, but even wearing them he still kept his gaze averted from the trapdoor. 'No one gets this far. I can't believe you missed the crocodile swamp. Anyone who's got a way off this place generally takes it at the writhing maggots.'

'Put that thing down,' said the Doctor. 'Put it down. I. . . I beg you.'

'Well, I would have begged you not to try and cause a robot revolution, but you wouldn't have listened,' said Etienne, indistinctly as he continued to crunch through the plastic shell of the remote.

The Doctor turned away from him in disgust and ran towards Clara. She was already walking out of the door into the space beyond as if sleepwalking. Etienne's barking laughter echoed in the Doctor's ears, but Clara heard none of it.

Outside, the sunlight was golden like honey, the grass lusciously green and thick. They were on a path, looking ahead at a hill at the top of which was a vibrant orchard, with a wrought-iron fence around it. There was a gate, but it was open.

Clara ran towards it at full pelt, light of foot and joyous of heart. Inside were apple trees, but the apples were silver and gold. Their scent filled the air; Clara had never in her life felt such utter thirst, such terrible hunger. She ran, the Doctor arriving behind her, just as she stretched out her hand.

'Cla—'

The snake in this tree was green.

'Don't you *see* what this is?'

Small, jade-coloured, like a slithering jewel, the snake raised its head. Clara jumped back, but not for long. Her hunger drove her forwards. The Doctor shook his head and grabbed her shoulders. She struggled against him.

'Why on earth are you taking that form?' the Doctor shouted towards the snake.

The snake flickered its tongue at him. 'Hello again,' it said. 'Yes, well, rather. I got it from the human. Between that and your documented fondness for the species, I thought it might rather work.'

The Doctor looked wounded. 'Well, don't get me wrong, I like them and everything, but I've just spent thirty-five years working with the Sculptor Dwarves, and nobody ever mentions that.'

The snake indicated Clara. 'Well, anyway, it's in her head. Got it off the psychic wavelength that's running those poor robots.'

'People,' said the Doctor quickly.

'Something about... "Sunday school"?' said the snake. 'A little church room, a nice lady teacher, the smell of oak polish and the felt-tip colouring on the wall. She loved it.'

It coiled sinuously round a branch, rustling the thick, luxurious leaves.

The Doctor looked at Clara in surprise, then redoubled his grip as she kept trying to pull away from him.

'Nonetheless,' said the snake, stretching its neck in the sunlight. 'It is a rather beguiling look, don't you think? If only I could smell.'

'You're not having her,' said the Doctor, clinging on to Clara for dear life. She struggled against him, her feet trying to move of their own accord. 'You're not.'

The snake shimmered, its scales lost in the light. 'But would you deny her everything? Come, my daughter. Come, taste it all. Every single thing, every last delight, everything there ever was to know or to understand; the fruit of knowledge, of everything. Doesn't that sound delicious? You will love it.'

'It is not what he promises,' hissed the Doctor in Clara's ear, but she could not hear him.

'I want it,' she said. 'I am naked without it.'

'You aren't naked.' The Doctor tugged her again, but she didn't listen to him or even look at him.

'He doesn't know everything about you, does he?' said the snake. 'He doesn't really know you at all, does he? Doesn't know how you bleed for him. But what would he do for you? Does he bleed for you, pretty maid?'

'Clara,' the Doctor said. He glared at the snake, whose mouth was open, as if it were laughing. In desperation, the Doctor spun Clara round to face him, till she was forced to look at him, although her eyes strayed over his shoulder, her feet continued to move.

'I want it,' she said.

'But you have to work for it,' said the Doctor in anguish. 'You have to earn it.'

She shook her head. 'I *want* it.'

'You hate snakes, remember?'

Her eyes were glassy as she stared at him in confusion. It was as if she barely recognised him.

The snake reared and hissed crossly.

'Argh,' said the Doctor.

He held her by the shoulders, her eyes still desperately searching out the apples, her feet still leading her closer and closer to the orchard. The scent on the air now was completely soporific, lulling. It was very hard to think clearly.

With a huge effort, he spun her round to face him again, pushing them both fiercely back from the fence they were drifting towards, their feet not obeying their heads. With a massive effort of will, the Doctor shoved them away from the sharp iron posts so hard he tore both his hands in the process

'I have it,' he said, fast and intent. 'You know I do. I have it already. You can have it. You can have it. Just. . .' He glanced at the snake. 'Just, please. Take it from me.'

'He doesn't even care for you!' screamed the snake. 'He lets you bleed and you don't even know it! Will he bleed for you?'

The Doctor lifted his injured hands instinctively, and let the wounds show.

She hadn't even known his blood was red.

'Always,' he said simply.

They both watched as the drops fell, vivid on the bright green grass, forming a 'C'.

The second the first drop hit the ground, she snapped back to him.

'Stop that,' she said, looking directly at him at last. 'Stop it immediately.'

The Doctor reached out, gently, his fingers weaving into her dark hair. He had forgotten how small she was; she barely came up to his chest. 'Look at me,' he ordered sternly.

Reluctantly Clara focused her eyes on his.

'It is what you want, I promise.'

This was not quite a lie. He would show her the temptation and fruits of that knowledge; everything he had. But he would also show her what it cost and what it really meant and how, afterwards, the rest of her life would be like a dark, spoiled fruit. She could not do this. She was not capable; it would kill her. Or worse.

Etienne had been quite wrong. He had never tasted the fruit. He had never had to.

Her focus wavered.

'Clara! Look at me. Look at me. You have to let me in. You have to let me. You have to say yes.'

Finally, slowly, she blinked her assent and breathed 'Yes', and he pushed his fingers a little more firmly on the side of her head. A golden light started to flow between them as he moulded their selves together, concentrating on pushing to her an awareness of what was there, what he lived with, what the cost would be; how she must resist the temptation; she must.

Just as he was concentrating on the flow from his brain to hers, however, he stopped, and his eyes flicked open suddenly in surprise as, suddenly, he felt her: felt her self-knowledge buried so deeply underneath, so deep in her subconscious; but that showed what the snake had said was true.

She remembered so little, but it was there, deep in the bone; her frustration and her fear and her pain at being around him, all of it buried so far beneath the surface that she did not understand it herself.

Abruptly, shocked and startled, he jumped back as if electrified, and their connection instantly ceased, far too sharply. Clara crumpled underneath him like a paper doll.

The Doctor stared down at her, horrified, then instantly made use of the situation, grabbing her up in his arms and running for all his life, the sunlight softly glinting in his hair, the deep, corrupt, sweet scent of apples in the air, the shrieking, furious scream of the bright green snake. He tore back to the house of skulls, his heart in his mouth, his shock and incredible regret cluttering up his mind.

'Shut the door!' he yelled at Etienne as he entered.

But Etienne simply laughed and said, 'I thought I wasn't in charge any more,' and did not move his vast limbs away from where he was reprogramming the skeletons.

'*Shut it!*' The deadly sunlight was still streaming in. The Doctor look around for a hanging, a coat, anything, that could cover it, as Clara started to stir in his arms. The light lit up every dark corridor, every grim corner flushing out its secrets to the bright golden glorious flood of tempting rays.

'There it is!' said Etienne, raising his fingers from the screen. 'The robots are all fixed. I am a genius. Guards! Take them!'

There was a rattling noise. The tallest of the skeletons, the one they had first seen on the cliff's edge, came marching into the room, followed by another, then another, then another. The Doctor stood up, carefully. Etienne laughed in triumph.

But instead of seizing the Doctor and Clara, the skeleton did something quite different: he led them up to the door's edge, and slowly laid himself down. Etienne pressed a button on the console and the skeleton spasmed as the white light flashed up and down, but it did not stop what it was doing. Another lay down on top of him, then another and another even as they were shocked, again and again, and Etienne screamed at them, until gradually they filled up the space, every chink, and the light died down and down until it vanished completely.

Clara lay on the floor, her eyes flickering. Eventually she came to, blinking. She looked around the room. 'What happened here?' she asked, gazing at the pile of bones.

Etienne and the Doctor stared at her. Then Etienne turned his attention to the Doctor.

'Those worthless bits of bone,' he growled. 'You utter idiot.'

'They're not worthless bits of bone!' said the Doctor furiously. 'Do you know they even try and warn people who land here? Leave them messages?'

Etienne shrugged. 'They're *robots*.'

'You tell yourself that.'

Etienne shook his head. 'But you came back to this place.'

The Doctor stared at the floor. 'I didn't know what it was then, either,' he said. 'It wasn't protected.'

'Chuh.' Etienne stood up, wheezing slightly. He was not tall. 'How do you stop it?' he asked, suddenly serious. 'How do you stop all that knowledge and that power from making you take over the galaxy? From making you destroy it all? From making you an eater of worlds? How do you stop it?'

The Doctor was still staring quietly at the ground. 'I work at it. Very, very hard. All the time. Every day. And I don't always.'

Etienne gave that maddening grin again. 'But you told the Shadow Proclamation it was here?'

The Doctor nodded.

'And then they "hired" me. Or they thought they did. To protect everybody else.'

The Doctor nodded again, very, very wearily.

Etienne watched him as he moved things into the room; much of the packet food, the water filter, every bit of computer equipment.

'What are you doing, man?' he said, nervous. 'You guys are leaving, right? I mean, you'll need me, right? You'll never get back alone, you'll need me to guide you – there's stuff out there you haven't even seen yet. There's stuff out there I don't even remember making. You gotta watch for that zombie ravine, it's hideous. They've got rakes for hands. Boy, I was out of it that night.'

At that, the Doctor marched forward without saying a word, took every handset and controller he could find, and crushed them under the heel of his boot. Then he went back to working quietly, saying nothing.

Etienne tried to leave the room, but more skeletons came to block his way. Sweating heavily, he turned round to try and reach his remote control, only to remember that the Doctor had it and it was now sticking out of his top pocket. His manifest unfitness made any attempt to launch himself at the Doctor or Clara laughably feeble, the heavy atmosphere in the room growing increasingly unpleasant. He gave up, and started to whine again.

'They're not real people! I didn't know they were! I just thought—'

The Doctor set down a final pile of blankets, apparently satisfied that was enough. 'You know,' he said, in a voice of great weariness and near infinite sorrow. 'You know I cannot let you free. To sit here, and wait for the deaths of others, and use their remains for your own ends. . . You have proven yourself too dangerous to be let loose on the universe.'

'They let *you* out,' said Etienne sourly.

'Here is everything you need. You will protect the drawbridge: the skeletons have done their duty well. You may build your little worlds, Etienne, on your computers; you can play in a virtual world till your heart's content, but you must never see sunlight again. I will deadlock seal this room.'

'Nooo!' said Etienne, tears now mingling with the sweat pouring down his face, his eyes darting all around looking for an escape route.

'You can take the drawbridge of course. . .'

Etienne shook his head frantically. 'No. No no no no.'

'Then we understand each other,' said the Doctor. 'Build virtual worlds of suffering. This one can no longer contain you.'

He moved over and spoke quietly to the skeletons piled by the drawbridge. They rattled once, twice. The

Doctor understood. He took out the remote control and, with a consoling hand on the uppermost skull, gently powered it down until they were, once more, simple piles of bones. Etienne, screaming in disbelief, followed it with his eyes, and the rest of them as they filed out, leaving him alone.

Outside, it didn't take much; a simple act of the sonic screwdriver to deadlock the door for ever. They could hear Etienne inside, cursing and yelling and screaming and banging on it; a toddler in a rage.

'But what about the... the tree,' said Clara, whose memories of exactly what had gone on were hazy and muddled. 'Isn't it round the back of the house?'

'Go look,' said the Doctor, and Clara did, even though it was dark and freezing and once more the empty, horrible windswept plain of before – and remained so, all the way around.

'Where is it?' she asked.

'Through his drawbridge, in that room,' said the Doctor. 'He always controlled the portal.'

'And won't he go through it?'

'He knows exactly what will happen if he does,' said the Doctor. 'The instant he takes a bite of that apple, the cold wind will blow and the sun will disappear and his mind will be full of the knowledge of a universe of pain and suffering and death, and he will have to live inside that mind a long, long time.'

He picked up one of the many loose pebbles then, and hurled it with some force at the horizon. This time, nothing rattled.

'Is that what you have?' Clara asked timidly.

He turned to her with a half-smile. 'Not quite,' he said. 'When you gain knowledge for yourself... when you see the universe and learn about its good and its bad... you get the fairy in the bottom of the box too. You see the whole picture, not just... the entropic chronicle of perpetuity.'

Clara was still thoughtful as they stepped out in the moonlight. 'Doctor. . .' she said nervously. 'What are you going to do with him?'

'Oh, I expect the Shadow Proclamation have been looking for him for a long time.' He stared back at the house, shaking his head.

'And, er, how are we going to get off this planet?'

The Doctor gave her a gentle smile. 'Very, very slowly and with great care.'

The Doctor was true to his word. First he gathered all of the remaining skeletons together. Then he sent them out with all the seedlings, to disseminate throughout the planet. He brought the bees and birds out of hyper-sleep and sent them forward to pollinate the seed, and recalibrated the weather centre to give them hyper-fast growing seasons, which meant it was rainy and sunny every five minutes it seemed to Clara, mostly wet.

Every time he emptied out a room, they dismantled the bones and buried them far and wide so they could fertilise the earth, until there were only two rooms left standing; Etienne's, which they gave a wide berth (it had gone very quiet: the Doctor suspected that Etienne had gone straight back into eating and playing with computers and wasn't necessarily having a much different experience to his life before, except now he was doing it virtually), and the library, tidied up, as a shelter from the rainfall.

The rain washed away the scree, and extraordinarily fast the plants began to sprout and take hold, spread about like a desert after rain. They grew up thick and fast. Some Clara had seen before: huge, sprawling bushes of bougainvillea, in thick pinks and purples, bright and popping against the pale blue sky between showers; willows that followed the rivulets of water; sunflowers that sprang up overnight and followed the path of the sun, a banana plantation the Doctor had insisted on. And others she didn't recognise; great yawning bushes that looked like sea anemones; flame-coloured trees in bright red. Every day the landscaped changed; the scents strong on the gentle morning breeze. Vines grew up and wrapped themselves around the two remaining rooms, almost concealing their grisly origins.

Clara sat shelling peas and glanced over at the Doctor, who had taken off his jacket in the sunshine, turned up his sleeves, and was whittling. He was humming a cheerful song of contentment as he did so. A light breeze was ruffling his hair, and she smiled involuntarily as she watched him. He looked up just at that moment and caught her eye and smiled back.

'What?'

Clara shook her head. 'It's just. . . I can't believe how peaceful it is here now.'

He held her gaze for a long moment. 'I know,' he said. 'But we have to move on.'

She nodded.

'And you. . .' he said. 'When I was in your head. . .'

Even though her memories were confused, she remembered glimpses; her inexplicable fury at the ravine, and her sense of him: of pity and of shame.

'Do you still feel like that?' he persisted, obviously uncomfortable with the conversation. 'About me, you know. About what we do. I mean, because, for me. Well. You know. Surprise! Ha!'

Clara picked her words carefully. 'I don't know,' she said, truthfully. 'Sometimes I feel that things are too hard. And sometimes I feel brave as a lion. But I don't know why. It's like a dream I had once, that's just out of reach. . . but it's always with me.'

'Because I can't. . . I can't be a *burden*.'

Clara looked at him in surprise. 'But burdens can be shared,' she said gently. 'And I am. . . I am. . .'

They were interrupted suddenly by one of the taller skeletons. The Doctor had found old identity passes and names scattered about one of the rooms, but there were so many, so many, and they had not been able to give anyone a name, or a grave.

The adult skeleton before them held up his finger to indicate that he wanted to talk, and the Doctor nodded. Clara came over to watch, as the ash scattered on the ground.

'O-N-E-T-H-I-N-G,' it said. 'T-H-E-N-G-O.'

The Doctor nodded respectfully. 'Of course,' he said. He took the skeleton's claw in his and held it carefully. 'Thank you.'

The skull nodded.

'What?' said Clara.

'Time to leave,' said the Doctor.

The Doctor made final adjustments to the weather station to set it on a smooth path; tidied up carefully, glanced not even once at the locked bone room sitting solitary.

'Why didn't they destroy this planet?' said Clara, as they started to move, following the long marching line of remaining skeletons, who travelled ahead. 'To have all the knowledge in the universe concentrated in such a small way. It's *so* dangerous. Any life form that takes it... it's dangerous for everyone. Wouldn't it be better just to destroy it?'

The Doctor shrugged. 'I don't know,' he said quietly. 'There may come a day when the universe needs that knowledge, when everybody needs it.'

'Who put it there?' said Clara.

'Oh, it has always been there,' said the Doctor. 'And I was just the unutterable, awful fool who told somebody.'

Clara patted his hand. 'But look at it now,' she said, indicating around them. The fresh earth and new moss was soft under her bare feet. The tangle of growth meant the world was a riot of green and cherry blossom; long avenues of new fruit trees, some flowering, some already dropping fruit, like all the seasons come at once.

'This you can have,' said the Doctor, handing her an apple, green and red. It was sweet and sharp all at once and its juices ran down her chin. 'Anyone that lands here now... I hope there will be so many orchards, they won't find that one in a hurry.'

'That's amazing,' she said, looking round. 'But what about all the monsters?'

The Doctor took Etienne's controller from his pocket. 'Quite handy having monsters you can turn on and off at will,' he said. 'Wish they were all like that. But there was only one monster, really.'

'And the big snakes?'

'Oh, they're real,' said the Doctor. 'But hopefully now we've established an ecosystem, they'll be able to survive in it without being half-starved to death and furious.'

'*Hopefully*,' said Clara, still eyeing the trees with some nervousness. But all she could see were brilliant parrots flitting from branch to branch and, from far off, something that sounded a little like the chattering of a monkey.

'You brought *monkeys*?'

'Come on,' said the Doctor. 'You don't grow this many bananas without letting in a few monkeys. That'd just be selfish.'

Finally they reached the large crevasse again that split the world in two, but it was unrecognisable. Now, a massive waterfall, formed from all the rainfall, fell over the side, a rainbow prism dancing off it. Below were fresh waters churning and bouncing, and Clara thought she saw a trout leap high in the sunlight.

The Doctor nodded to the skeleton, who moved forward and, with one superhuman jump, the white lights of the Carnutium filament flickering up and down his frame, landed on the other side. Then another, and another. And they joined hand to foot, and on the near side, the other skeletons joined, hand to foot, then, astonishingly, one figure staying on either side as an anchor, the two sides swung like trapeze artists, until they caught and held hands, and made a bridge.

'Oh my,' said Clara.

'Amazing stuff, Carnutium filament,' said the Doctor. 'He was a clever, clever chap indeed. Such a waste. But this is their last gift to us. And then we must set them free.'

The littlest skeleton was on the far side of the abyss, as the Doctor and Clara carefully picked their way across it. As he usually did, he ran to Clara for a cuddle, his mother not far behind.

Clara held him for a long time in her lap then stood up. 'This is what you all want?' she said.

The figures nodded, and those left behind on the far bank waved.

'To return to the earth,' said the Doctor. 'Where good can be done.'

Clara bestowed one last kiss on the bare white skull. '*Au revoir, mon bout-chou.*'

Then the Doctor took the remote from his pocket, still glowing bright white, and hurled it with all his strength into the abyss. It fell so far that no one heard it hit the bottom, but instantly, as if someone had cut the strings, the bones all collapsed to the ground, and were still.

'Thank you,' said the Doctor, and Clara, too, nodded.

They covered what they could in fresh flowers as a burial mound, then continued on, through a beautiful avenue that now opened up through the forest, daisies and mushrooms and snowdrops flourishing at the roots, fresh green leaves on every twig and branch. Clara felt a movement in the branches to her right, but she did not turn her head. She did, though, take the Doctor's hand.

The great expanses of sand had gone; instead, when they emerged from the forest, she saw they had been replaced by a wildflower meadow. Rabbits hopped through meadowsweet, sweet peas and waving daffodils. And straight across the plain, under a bower, Clara saw it, the TARDIS – the real, solid TARDIS; not an illusion this time, ringed round with newly sprung pink roses. She ran to it with a happy gasp, the Doctor very close behind her.

The Doctor plucked one of the beautiful blooms entwined around the door and, carefully, put it behind her ear. She flushed at his touch, then smiled.

'Senorita!' he said. 'Shall we go somewhere awesome? With a name and everything?'

'Heh. We should name this place.'

'No,' said the Doctor. 'We should not.'

Clara immediately plucked a rose of her own and, stretching up, tucked it behind his ear, then put her hands on her hips and regarded the results with a disappointed expression.

'Stick to hats?' said the Doctor.

'Definitely.'

'Just as well I look so good in all the hats,' he yelled, as he vanished inside the TARDIS.

Several minutes later he came back, with a small, heavy narrow replica of the TARDIS, about waist height, with a real telephone attached to it. Next to it was a sign that could be read in any language.

'If you have crash-landed here, call this number. Advice and Assistance Obtainable Immediately.'

It looked incongruous in the beautiful meadow. But also somehow quite right. He disappeared back inside.

Clara peered after him, then turned around and glanced one last time at the buzzing, green, sunlit world around her, as a butterfly passed her by on its merry way, its cream wings fluttering happily.

'I am... going to be fine,' she said to herself. And she briefly touched once more the rose in her hair, then slipped inside the TARDIS herself as the butterfly rose on a zephyr in the suddenly empty air, and flew up again and again, higher than the greenest treetops.

Picnic at Asgard

Monday 5 May 5147

Stormcage

'Oi!' was the first thing I heard.

This was a good sign. Definitely boded well. I risked cracking open an eyelid.

'What the blooming heck do you think you're doing?'

Trying not to throw up would have been the honest answer.

It was the Time Hopper. Traded it with Frodene in the showers for ninety-five sugar mice that had unaccountably arrived anonymously 4,600 years past their sell-by date; and an incredibly rare and holy protective relic Father Octavian sent me years ago, with a letter begging that I keep it by me always in my quest for true repentance. Frodene likes it glinting on her tail.

The Hopper can't get you past the Tesla force field, of course, but – if you're happy to stay in one place – amazingly, it works perfectly. Here I was, still in my cell, geographically perfect; but on the very day the cell was being built. The bars weren't even fitted yet.

'Where'd you spring from, then?'

I noticed the workman's surprised voice sounded slightly muffled, then realised to my annoyance that I couldn't breathe. They hadn't oxygenated the area yet. *So* annoying.

'Sorry! Gotta go!' I said in a slightly strangulated voice, quickstepping over his tools and stopping merely to grab his keycard and his oxygen supply.

I am almost one hundred per cent sure... maybe seventy-nine per cent sure... that one of his colleagues would have got to him with back-up oxygen in time.

And after that, we would both need a day off.

Asgard

He was waiting, arms folded, leaning against the TARDIS, pretending he wasn't fidgeting. He hates waiting. If he's not arriving in the nick of time, it isn't worth it.

'Come on!' he said. 'It's open and everything! We're missing it!'

'Hello, Sweetie.'

'I thought,' he said, unfolding his arms, 'you only called people that when you couldn't remember their names.'

'Not true,' I replied, ditching the stolen helmet. 'It's also if I can't remember their gender. Anyway, I had to stop at the market.'

He looked dubiously at the wicker basket I'd brought. 'What are we having to eat?'

'Stop being fussy.'

'I just want to—'

'No,' I said firmly. 'If you're picking the location, I'm picking the food. And, by the way, the location is *ridiculous*.'

He turned round, gleefully, the vast golden gates spread out before us, shining like mad in the morning sun. 'Isn't it?!'

ASGARD™. A planet-sized theme park. It is ridiculous. Beyond ridiculous. 'A celebration of all things legendary.' The skies were a heaving, rolling pink, always with a strategic ray of sun bursting through triumphantly; you could take part in a great fire funeral, or join the Beating Tunnel Ship of 10,000 Drums ride; or fly mechanical eagles through thrilling rock falls. They have a 5,000-metre waterfall with a hotel built into the cave behind it that's lit entirely by naturally occurring prisms.

'This place is so tacky,' I said, as we walked through the vast bright shining gates towards the Rainbow Bridge, with thousands of other excited-looking tourists; children bubbling with excitement, wearing their toy winged helmets and brandishing bendy hammers indiscriminately and then being told off for it.

'Don't anger the Gods!'

'Are you going to be like this all day?'

I nudged at him to look at the family near us. They were Pharax. Blue, at any rate. Three parents, and a clutch of children at various stages, including one nearly fully grown, and obviously a teenager. His clothes were ill-fitting and drooped, and he slouched, as much as a flint exoskeleton could slouch.

The lad's expression showed plainly how annoyed he was at being dragged here, even as his younger siblings bounced and hopped cheerfully round his feet and pointed at things they wanted to buy later. And he kept taking out an electronic device, whereupon one of his parents would tell him to put it away and he would scowl and do it reluctantly.

'Teenagers are the same in every galaxy,' I said.

'I know,' said the Doctor, smiling. 'Brilliant.'

And there was a slight pause. And I told myself sternly I wasn't bringing it up.

'Certainly, sir, madam,' the attendant in the booth was saying, as the Doctor waggled the psychic paper at him. 'It's a great honour to have you here today. Let me make sure you have VIP passes to everything. Gets you to the front of all the rides.'

'Oh,' said the Doctor, looking wounded. 'Oh, no, I mean, we would *never* push in in a queue.'

'Doctor!' I hissed. 'I'm not waiting for hours to go on stupid rides! Take the passes!'

'But it's not fair!' he said.

The attendant was beginning to look suspicious, which always has a wobbly effect on psychic paper.

'Just take them!' I said.

'And your complimentary horned helmets!' offered the attendant.

'No, thank you,' I said, at the exact same second the Doctor said, 'Cool!'

We joined the hordes of day-trippers streaming onto the Rainbow Bridge.

'I'm not skipping the queues, though,' he said mutinously.

'I know,' I said. 'That's why I brought a book.'

Still, you would have had to be a lot more churlish than me – and have spent a lot less time staring at a brick wall – not to be impressed by the Rainbow Bridge.

This area of the park was always a stunning gold and pink dawn, fresh fingers of the sun warming your shoulders; and a 5,000-piece orchestra played you across on great swells of sublime music. You could glimpse the endless waterfall in the distance, but the river below was wild and deep and clear and looked like the most refreshing, cold and delicious thing ever, like liquid sunlight. (They had glasses of it for sale at a concession stand, so you could find out – for an exorbitant fee.) Still, you really did feel like you were leaving one world behind, and I smiled, feeling quite excited.

'I'm not doing the mining,' I warned him.

'Come on! "Join 5,000 trolls digging for real gold and diamonds in a hundred real mountain tunnels a mere eagle ride away!"' the Doctor read from the map. 'What's not fun about that?'

'You're forgetting I only narrowly avoided the hard labour mines...' I began, but he'd gone. I glanced around. He'd better not be looking for trouble. This was not the day for that. Plus, I had to talk to him about ...

I spotted him by the stone sides of the bridge, kneeling in front of a very small rotund humanoid child, who was sobbing inconsolably.

'It's OK,' he was saying. 'You're not lost. Well, not for long. Nobody can stay lost for long. Not when I'm about. Here, look at this.'

He took his screwdriver out and made it shoot tiny coloured fireworks in the air. Which I had thought was a waste of space when he did the modification, so shows all I know.

The child's eyes widened and it reached up a sticky hand.

'I know, it's my favourite, too,' said the Doctor. 'But don't touch. What's your mother's name? Do you know?'

'Mama,' said the child.

'Yes,' said the Doctor. 'Good start. Got anything else to go on?'

'Want Mama!'

'Let me just programme this to get a DNA trace—'

The child grabbed hold of the sonic very tightly and refused to let it go.

'The thing is, if you give it back to me, I can find your mama.'

'Find Mama!' ordered the child. 'Give LIGHTS ME! ME LIGHTS!'

'Let me just. . .' said the Doctor, switching the fireworks setting off.

'WAAAAH!!!!' The child screamed fit to wake the dead.

Suddenly a vast lumbering mountain of a person huffed over and grabbed the child by the hand.

'Mure! There are you are! Oi! What the blooming heck do you think you're doing?'

I was hearing that a lot today.

'Well, your child was lost, and I was—'

'He ain't lost!'

'But I was—'

'WANT LIGHT MAMMA!!!!'

'Give him that light, then.'

'But I was. . .'

'GIVE IT.'

'Manners. . .' said the Doctor weakly.

I stepped out in front. 'Excuse me,' I said, in a voice I have known to get excellent results. 'Were you planning to join in the funeral pyre ritual later? Because if you weren't, I'd be quite happy to facilitate it.'

'*River*,' said the Doctor.

The woman looked at me, sizing me up.

I smiled broadly, and pulled back my coat to give her a quick glimpse of my prison tattoo. (It's temporary: I needed to gain Frodene's trust. Well, I *hope* it's temporary.)

The woman balked and backed away. 'Well, you can see who wears the trousers with you two,' she spat, marching away. 'Come on, Mure.'

'What's wrong with wearing trousers?' asked the Doctor, puzzled. He said goodbye sweetly to the child, who was being roughly hauled away, great big puddles of bright snot pooling on his upper lip.

'Want light,' the boy hiccupped sadly, looking over his shoulder, as his mother shook him roughly, then jammed some sweets in his mouth.

I wondered. Now? Should I do it now? I couldn't stop thinking about it. This would have been the moment, I know. To ask him. Asking the Doctor for advice on my personal life. Oh lord, I have had better ideas.

The thing is, normally I love making him laugh, when I do things he wouldn't. But I am never truly as brave as I pretend to be, and, actually, I have a theory that he is absolutely the only creature in the universe who is.

Regardless: I couldn't bear the idea of him laughing *at* me.

I couldn't bear it. After all, with my childhood. . . imagine, me. The very idea of raising a child. Absurd. Who would leave a child with someone as dangerous as me? How would I have the faintest idea what to do: I who had known absolutely nothing of parenting. How could I tuck a child into bed?

And what if he thought I was asking him? That would be ridiculous. Completely stupid.

After all, what kind of father would he make anyway? He lives in the moment, only for today. That's what children do, not what they need. They need utter repetitive boredom, day after day after day, life exactly the same; a great big net of boring: of boring old love and times tables and vegetables. Nothing we could even begin to provide.

But if not now, when? Because I am not getting any younger.

Because he is.

Not that I am thinking about that.

'Hey!' I said, as something landed on my hair.

'You looked distracted!'

'That is absolutely no reason to fasten a helmet on me!'

'Chill out, Brunhilde!' the Doctor said. 'Now, there was a girl. . .'

'You know, Vikings didn't really wear horns on their helmets.'

'Mythic ones did,' he said, marching off, and the moment was gone.

The main square of Asgard™ was heaving; everywhere were half-timbered buildings; a working smithy –

huge – where you could get weapons hammered into shape, or jewellery; there were bakeries selling honey cakes, and, obviously mead stalls everywhere. The Doctor couldn't stay still, zooming from one side of the square to another, cheerfully replying 'Hello!' back to grinning people who were clearly just being paid to say hello: it was all the same to him.

'Starting shortly in the Valhalla Amphitheatre: the fearsome Dragon Wars of Thor,' came a booming over the loudspeaker system. The crowds started to move in that direction.

'Ooh,' said the Doctor, looking at me expectantly.

'How can you *possibly* want to watch a fake animatronic monster show?' I said in disbelief.

'Are you kidding? Somewhere people are screaming at a monster and I don't have to do anything? Tremendous! Scream away! I shall have my feet up on the seat in front. Unless they tell me not to.'

And he led on, exuberantly. I wouldn't have told him so in a million years, but he rather suited the helmet.

The vast amphitheatre was crowded with people from all over the galaxy. I couldn't work out what the strange thing was I was feeling; then I realised. It was normality. Going to a theme park. For fun. With someone you cared about. Being hideously gouged for mead. I was enjoying all of it.

We were ushered to special VIP seats front and centre.

'VIP sucks!' shouted someone behind us, and we both looked embarrassed and agreed. I looked round. It was the grumpy teenager from before.

One of his triparents was trying to admonish him. I overheard him say, 'Well, if you hate all this stuff so much, you're more than welcome to go and get a job, Tomith.'

'Yeah, and end up like you?' The teenager sniffed and buried his head back in his device, completely ignoring what was taking place in front of him.

Which was a shame, as I have to admit, I have seen some sights, but the Asgard™ dragon show was quite the most spectacular.

First the orchestra played their most stirring music – and if you have never heard 3,000 violins play in harmony, I recommend it – then due to some clever atmospheric tweaking, the sun suddenly set above our heads in a million glowing shades of pink and purple streaking across a golden sky. As the stars popped out above us, thousands and thousands of tiny candles lit themselves, until the amphitheatre was a glittering fairyland and a collective 'ooo' could be heard from the crowd.

I realised we were holding hands, but we weren't running.

A man brandishing a huge sword ran onto the floor of the amphitheatre, holding up his weapon. He looked tiny down there. Then behind him came more and more and more; as the orchestra beat the drums, an entire army emerged, standards raised, marching in perfect unison to the music; it was oddly stirring, as thousands of them lined up, displaying their marching skills. Then the music changed, and lots of women ran on too, with long plaits and beautiful embroidered garments, and the entire arena erupted into a victory war dance around the campfires which sprang up suddenly.

Then just as we were lulled into the display, a single person, dressed in furs, tore onto the floor. He could have been an interloper, except for his sword, and he shouted loudly about a dragon, a dragon coming this way, whereupon the actors dissolved their dancing and made a huge line; brought out their weapons which all burst into huge lines of flame above their head, and the music changed to something ominous and scary.

There was a long pause and then a great noise, like a huge metal foot striking the ground.

'Oooh!' said the Doctor. 'What's that?'

There was another sound, then another, then another from near the entrance. The crowd of performers shrank back, and so did the audience. And when the burst of flame appeared, everybody jumped. It was immense; we could feel the heat from up in the box.

'Whoa!' said the Doctor.

Then BOOM you could just see, entering the arena, one huge metal claw. The ground shook. Then another, then another; clang clang clang. The Doctor was gripping me in excitement. Then there was a huge cloud of smoke across the arena and when it cleared, the creature was there, at least four storeys high; a genuine metal monstrosity, shaped like a dragon, with huge bright red glowing eyes. It opened its sharp jaws wide to the sky and an enormous roar and a billowing flame erupted.

The beast rampaged around the stadium floor, causing the performers to cower in terror; occasionally approaching a bank of the audience. At one point it reached out a surprisingly delicate claw and lifted a hat off someone, to vast applause.

Then the mood darkened again; the people on stage cowered, and in another puff of smoke, from the entrance appeared a man – a huge man, blond of hair and beard, incredibly over-muscled (*some* might say), dressed in chainmail and a loin cloth, with a hammer the size of me, marched into the arena to a huge and overwhelming standing ovation from the audience.

'Why do I never get one of those?' came the voice to my left.

'Sssh,' I said. 'It's just getting interesting. He's very oily.'

'Fierce and mighty dragon!' shouted Thor, amplified throughout the arena. 'Face me in combat!'

The dragon turned round, its red eyes blinking, smoke puffing from its giant nostrils. With a roar it pawed the ground and prepared to charge. Thor stood his ground. It looked a ridiculously uneven fight, as the dragon backed the man into a corner, whereupon Thor struck the weapon with an almighty clank, and harmless green sparks showered the first ten rows. He swung it round with some rather unnecessary pyrotechnics, then whacked it straight into the head of the dragon, which staggered backwards, then regrouped to run at him again. But now Thor was a blur of motion; spinning and hacking; at one stage seemingly cornered, then rolling out from underneath the creature; temporarily losing his sword, but not before he'd hacked off a great sharp-needled toe from the dragon and was fighting him off with his own pointed nail, etc. It was all very stirring stuff; the dragon veered almost but not too dangerously close to the crowd; just at the last minute, the flames wouldn't quite reach, or the claws would draw back, as the audience screamed.

Thor was gearing up for the very last charge; the audience in a frenzy. He had escaped near-death several times now and the crowd was absolutely ready for the kill. He advanced slowly on the puffing, bucking, crazed animatronic beast.

And then something strange happened. The tail of the dragon went over the side of the barrier, and knocked an entire row off their seats. A great screaming broke out. The huge beast wobbled and wavered as if about to topple over, and absolute panic broke out in the stands. We both stayed watching closely, neither of us sure whether or not this was all part of the act; perhaps that section of the audience were stooges, to make the experience more intense for the spectators. Then the Doctor grabbed my arm.

'Look,' he said.

The dragon was now twirling around, its robotic limbs flailing everywhere, and it had inadvertently scooped up a figure from the stands.

It was a child; the same child we'd found earlier, wandering free from its parents. It had clearly been wandering free again, and had got onto a very dangerous path.

The dragon lurched, holding the tiny child – who looked even tinier in its claws – as the audience screamed and gasped.

'Quick...' I said, turning, but of course the Doctor had already gone.

There must have been a control room somewhere, because the dragon lurched to the left and to the right as there was a frantic struggle for control. And as people started to dangerously cram themselves towards the exits in panic, and the actors vanished, I saw a lone lanky figure down on the floor of the amphitheatre, waving his arms.

The beast was a robot of course, it had no independent thought at all, but it responded to movement and noise. I ran down the steps towards the stage and clambered over the barriers. Security had vanished, which was a tad disappointing. Perhaps all that smiling had tired them out.

The Doctor was trying to get close to it, but every time he approached, the dragon would drop its head and make a lunging noise, just as it was programmed to do so with Thor, who was, I noticed disapprovingly, huddled in a side entrance, pressed against the wall, terrified. He'd left his hammer discarded in the middle of the stage.

'I'll distract it!' I shouted, hoping the hammer would have a trigger effect on the robot, which it did. I couldn't lift it, but I could waggle it from side to side. The robot turned its mighty head towards me.

'Give him one of your looks,' came the Doctor's voice as he charged round the back of the great beast and tried to grab it by the tail, which lashed furiously.

The child was screaming, but seemed to be being held quite securely. I didn't have a hope of reaching up there, and wished I still had my trusty lasso. Instead, I glanced around. There were stones on the ground, surrounding the facsimile campfires. I picked them up and tried to figure out where to throw them that wouldn't hit the howling boy. I aimed for the knees, which seemed to work; the creature started to unbalance slightly, leaning, then overreaching.

'Again!' shouted the Doctor.

I let loose and the great tail came crashing down for long enough for him to grab hold of it. He clambered up it, carefully, as I stopped throwing stones – I didn't want the beast to fall with the two of them on it, and instead ran underneath, trying to work out where best to place myself if I had to catch the child.

The Doctor was now hoisting himself up the underside of the creature's tail, so it looked as if he were hanging off a giant branch, and was pulling himself hand over hand.

'Help!' the woman was screaming from the sidelines. 'GET MY BABY!'

I watched the Doctor and the boy anxiously, adrenalin pounding, as the Doctor shouted, 'Right! On my count, River, be ready!'

And with an almighty lunge, he let go with both hands, with only his legs clinging on to the rampaging creature's tail, and hurled himself backwards. The creature lurched, the leg I'd damaged moving up in the air – then, crack, there was the noise of a great switch being flicked, and the huge beast froze.

So did everybody fleeing for the exits. A momentary hush descended. But not for long.

There was an ominous creak. I held my breath. And the great four-storey creature twitched, just a little. And the leg I had whacked with stones started to tremble. It was like watching a tree being cut down.

The great stampede of people turned tail yet again and fled for the exits. We, on the other hand, could do nothing but stand and watch.

I drew a deep breath and stood as tall as I was able. Then I shouted at the child: 'Mure! Mure! Can you jump?'

The kid gazed at me with terrified eyes, shaking his head tightly.

'Jump to me,' I said. 'Come on, sweetie. You can do it.'

He shook his head mutely. The beast's leg trembled again. Inside there was a twisting noise of crunching metal. Something was going terribly wrong in there.

'You have to!' I said. 'Come on, Mure. You have to. Just do it!'

He shook his head again.

'Come on!' I shouted desperately. 'Come on! You can do it!'

The little boy edged slightly closer to the edge of the creature's great claws.

'That's right!' I said. 'Come on! I know you're very brave, and I'm going to catch you!'

He inched forwards a tiny bit more, and I smiled encouragingly.

'Come on!'

He was ready, his hands going up.

Suddenly his mother was by my side.

'MURE!' she screamed. 'GET DOWN HERE! GET DOWN RIGHT NOW!'

This had the opposite effect. The child shrank back into himself straightaway.

'NOW!'

The headshaking had recommenced. I glanced at the beast. Yes, the creaking was getting louder. The beast was starting to lean further and further over. I held my hands out even higher for the child.

'Mure. Please,' I said. It was such a long drop, and he was such a small child.

'*River!* Use this!'

The Doctor was sliding down the creature's tail, which had the unavoidable effect of unbalancing the beast completely. As he did so, he hurled his sonic high in the air, and it curled over the dragon's flanks and flew straight towards me.

I caught it in my left hand, and switched it up; the fireworks began to dance lightly from the end.

'Look, Mure!' I said. 'Look!'

And the huge beast began to topple, just as the little boy gazed at the fireworks, and shouted 'Lights!', and the Doctor leapt first, and was there supporting me, just as Mure leapt into my arms, as the robot landed on the arena floor with a crash that shook the earth.

Mure propelled us both back onto his mother, who took more than the brunt of it, but neither of them cared; she grabbed the child and smothered him in a mixture of hard hugs and kisses. The huge robot lay motionless and lifeless, half a section of seats completely squashed beneath it.

'Thank you, River and Doctor, for saving my baby,' said the Doctor pointedly.

'You're very welcome, polite and attentive parent,' I said, dusting myself down. 'You know, I think I'm going to leave it to you to retrieve the screwdriver.'

Outside, there were people screaming and rushing for the exits. We marched through them, looking for the Command Centre. We found it behind another beautiful village square, with its thatched roofs and half-timbered tumbledown houses and picturesque blondes performing an apparently traditional dance which involved quite a lot more exposed flesh that one would expected that far up in a planet's northern hemisphere, but that's a post-Earthly fantasy paradise for you.

If you crept round the back of the town square, though, there was a high thicket of trees, facilities for a variety of biologies; and a very small, unsignposted path. We looked at one another and nodded.

The Command Centre was an unobtrusive grey bunker, without windows, and several control panels on the roof. There was a keypad by the door and as we approached, several dark-suited people marched sharply up towards it and keyed it open, and we simply slunk in behind them.

Inside was a vast space down a flight of stairs; it must have extended underneath the park. Which made sense. Indeed as I looked around the huge underground control centre I saw, amongst myriad screens and working computers – and a big smiling 3D picture of Thor exhorting the staff to 'FIGHT WIN SMILE!' – were long tunnels, careering off everywhere, with little white travel cable pods, moving at remarkable speeds, delivering Vikings, dancers, cleaners, catering staff, who waited for the subway system like oddly dressed commuters, presumably so nobody had to watch Thor queue for the toilet. It was quite a sight.

'Who are you?' said an unfriendly voice. I looked up. The voice belonged to a species I didn't recognise, but looked a bit like a beaver. It was humanoid size though, and stood on two stilt-like legs, it was kind of cross and cute-looking all at once.

'Hullo!' said the Doctor. 'We're on the VIP tour! This bit's great!'

'No you're not,' said the beaver. An outbreak of shouting was taking place over by a bank of monitors. 'Now, clear out, this is a restricted area.'

He folded his tiny paws, not very impressively, although his expression was serious, as was the blaster tucked into the pocket of his frankly adorable beaver overalls.

'Out!'

The commotion got louder.

'Did you see those guys on the screen?' came a voice. A smaller, greyer creature – more mole-like, although with the same augmented limbs – came clattering over. 'They saved a kid in the crowd! We should give them an award or something. Actually, you know what, boss, having an event that almost goes horribly wrong and then comes good at the last minute... that might be an idea you know. Might add a good level of jeopardy to the crowd...'

HIs voice petered out as he took us in standing in front of him.

'And here you are!'

'It's a small world, after all,' said the Doctor.

'Well done, you guys.'

The beaver scowled and reviewed the monitors. 'Was that you?'

'Saved the day!' said the Doctor. 'Where were security, by the way?'

The beaver frowned. 'Helping people towards the exits. Preventing a panic. Exactly what they're meant to be doing.'

The beaver, the mole and I peered round the cavern. People were yelling and dashing around.

'Glad to see there's no more panic. . . I'm the Doctor, by the way.'

'And I'm the Professor,' I said, smiling politely.

'So. What happened to your dragon?' asked the Doctor.

The beaver sniffed. 'I'm Caius Roose. Park Director,' he said. 'And it's nothing to worry about. Small mechanical failure. All fixed now.' He glanced at me. 'Are you one of the Brunhildes?'

'Enough of that.'

'Cause you sound just like her.'

The Doctor looked around. 'Are you going to close the park?'

Caius shook his head. 'Naw, just a minor technical issue. No one got hurt.'

'We should close it,' said the mole. 'Double-check everything.'

'I agree,' said the Doctor.

Caius scratched his head. 'We can't,' he said. 'It's our busiest time in the year. We close the park, we lose our profits, then next thing you know word gets out we're dangerous, and before you know it everyone stays away and we're out of business.'

'Maybe that's because you *are* dangerous,' I said.

'It's one mechanical failure,' muttered Caius again.

'We should still failsafe,' said the mole.

Caius turned on him. 'Postumus Fearne!' he said, exasperated.

'I'm just saying!' said the Mole.

'How many kids you got at home, Postumus?'

'Eleven,' said Postumus fondly.

'Right. And what are they going to eat when they find out Daddy's lost his job?' Caius turned back to us. 'There's 76,000 people work in Asgard™.'

He gestured a paw towards the long lines of people queuing for the subway trains, scooping them away, another tired-looking horde alighting as the cars stopped.

'It's a major source of employment in a very depressed part of the galaxy. And I'm responsible for them.'

'And for them,' said the Doctor, showing the screens that covered all of the park. Everywhere were happy youngsters out strolling with their families; with horned shaped balloons; babies in buggies; people having wonderful days in the sunshine.

'That's right,' said Caius. 'And look: there's no panic. Because everything is fine. And we'll investigate the mechanical fault and then everything can carry on just as it was.'

He looked around.

'I have the finest team in the galaxy, Doctor,' he said. 'Thanks for your help just now, but I'm not shutting this place down and sending them out to starve without a very good reason. Off with you now please. I only ask nicely once.'

Postumus showed us the door. His whiskers looked defeated.

'Postumus... do *you* think it's just a mechanical failure?' asked the Doctor quietly on the way.

Postumus glanced around. 'That should... it just shouldn't happen,' he said. 'I mean, it's the most sophisticated technology available. Should be unbreakable. I mean, it wouldn't just be an error. It wouldn't.' He fingered the pens in the top pocket of his dungarees. 'It's not how we do things at Asgard™,' he said. 'It just isn't. This is the happiest place in the galaxy.'

The Doctor raised an eyebrow. 'Now, where have I heard that before?'

Postumus accompanied us out the back way, and we emerged into the more sublime landscape of the park at large. We blinked in what was once again bright mid-afternoon sunshine. Above us circled lazy great golden eagles, which could be harnessed and ridden; ahead, grazing in a beautiful, endless elysian fields were the winged white Valkyrie horses, saddled up at night for the spectacular northern lights display that ended each day at the park.

There were signposts to the 'Enchanted Forest' ahead that led to, eventually, the great feasting halls of Valhalla, that supplied mead and sweetmeats at any hour of the day or night.

The Doctor looked back at the small door to the Command Centre, even now fading away between the trees.

'Those subways... they go all round the park, right?'
Postumus nodded.

'So if we wanted to get in and have a better look without Caius setting any furry goons on us...'

Postumus looked even more worried. 'Look,' he said. 'He's tough, but he's a good boss, Caius. I wouldn't want to get into trouble or anything.'

'No, no, I realise that,' said the Doctor. 'But you think there's something wrong, don't you?'

Postumus nodded. 'Try under the great feasting halls of Valhalla,' he whispered. 'There's so many caterers and performers coming out of there all hours of the day and night, they'd barely notice you. Especially you...' He pointed at me. 'All you need is the metal breastplate.'

'*I don't look like...*' I started, as the Doctor smiled triumphantly, and I gave up. Instead, we set off towards the Enchanted Forest through the once more cheerful throng.

Following the path through the forest was curious. Firstly, no matter how many thousands of people approached the narrow dirt path at the same time, as soon as you entered the trees, everyone was completely dispersed so you couldn't see anyone in front or behind you; you felt completely alone.

Secondly, we entered the forest in early summer, hot yellow sun filtering through bright young green leaves, waterfalls tinkling with snow melt; and timid fawns scampering out of our way as we approached; but as we progressed, the leaves turned a darker and darker green, then began to coil up into themselves; to turn bright shades of yellow, red and orange; then they started to tumble down off the trees, and grouse took off into the sky, and the air became crisper, with the scent of bonfires in the air, and the sun turned mellow and golden and mists coiled along the bottom of the leaf- strewn path, as we kicked our way through them, speaking of what might have gone wrong with the park, and this and that, and he lent me his elbow, and I took it.

Do it, I told myself. Do it now. We were perfectly alone, perfectly peaceful. And the crunching leaves beneath my leather boots had turned, I noticed, to crunching snow, and the air was suddenly twilight and chill, the first flakes, now, swirling down, two snow-geese taking off above our heads, silhouetted against a newly minted moon; and I leaned in closer to him – he never feels the cold.

Just ask him, I told myself. It's not like he's not used to questions.

'Oh, look over there!' he said suddenly, just as I opened my mouth to speak. A gap in the trees had appeared, and I could see the snow-capped mountains of Asgard to the North – floodlit, and filled with gleeful skiers careening downhill, shouting and yelling in excitement.

'I've always wanted to try that. I should think I'd be very good.'

I burst out laughing. 'Don't be daft, your centre of gravity is far too high. You'd look like Crazy Legs the Crane. Anyway,' I continued. 'Look, there's something. . . something I need to ask you, and I don't even know if it's theoretically possible, and it's not even about you. . . probably. . . but if you thought no I need to see how that feels, and if it's yes I'd need to see how that feels, but I just need to ask, just once, and I have no one else to ask and. . . Do you think one day. . . I mean. . . I mean, one time. Do you think we. . . I. . . I might. . . do you think I might ever. . .'

Then there was a small blip, like I'd blinked a moment too long, and suddenly he was brushing snow off his jacket shoulders.

'Sorry,' he said. 'Lost concentration for a sec. What were you saying?'

I dropped his arm and stared at him. 'What did you just do?'

'Nothing.'

Something glinted inside his jacket. I grabbed at it.

'What's this?'

It was a gold medal. Inscribed on it was 'Helsinki, 1952'.

I looked at him for a long time.

'So what were you going to ask me?'

'Nothing,' I said. 'Forget it.'

I stomped off through the blizzard.

'Hang on, River!' he shouted after me. 'I can't run, my knees are shot.'

I did not 'hang on' and was almost out of the forest. Already I could see the braziers lighting the way to the palace of Valhalla up ahead, sending their flames high into the night.

And I could hear screaming.

The Palace of Valhalla looked like an optical illusion, because it was. It was tower upon tower, in thick grey granite; it resembled a great cathedral organ. Hundreds of windows were lit with thousands of glittering candles; you could enter any one of the 540 huge wooden doors.

I couldn't figure out where the screaming was coming from. A great smell of roasting meat and mead came towards us. I didn't notice this at first; for I was also dealing with the confirmation of something I knew all along: of course neither of us was remotely fit for parenthood. And I was an idiot even for thinking it, and wouldn't again.

We ran along the frosted path to the bottom of one of the towers. A girl in a metal breastplate lay unconscious on the ground; still breathing. She had the white cloak of one of the Valkyries; she was very young, and heavily made up. Her long wig lay in the snow. I knelt beside her, but as I did so, a troupe of security rushed up with a stretcher and erected a tent around her. 'Move along, please, she's fine, she's fine,' said a large mouse-like creature bossily. 'Just an accident. We do warn people not to run on the battlements.'

In an instant, she was whisked away, into one of the many doors in the walls.

'Another accident, huh?' said the Doctor. 'It does seem very careless, this place.'

We followed through the door through which they'd just disappeared; but we found ourselves in a huge hall, with only one set of doors.

I couldn't see how a stretcher could possibly have just come through here: inside, everyone was partying. The room was obviously an inter-dimensional trick: it contained a great long wooden table that went on for so far, the sightlines converged.

Everywhere along it were different families and groups together, eating, drinking happily, laughing and of course, making great toasts. Every so often there were huge fireplaces, above which meat was turning on spits, covered in herbs. Serving staff refilled goblets from huge, never-ending pitchers of mead.

'Ah,' said the Doctor.

He walked out, then came in again.

'What did you do that for?'

'No,' he said, gloomily. 'I came in a different door. Try it.'

I did so, and found myself exactly where I'd just been standing.

'A dimensional extension,' he said. 'Well, how else would you feed half a million visitors an hour, and make them all feel they're in the same great hall? They'll have gone somewhere else altogether.' He looked round. 'Something's very wrong here. What is it? Let me think.' He lifted a goblet of mead from a passing tray, drank it in one, then made a face.

'*Sip* stuff if you don't know you're going to like it!' I said crossly. I was about to try one for myself when one of the serving girls came running up to me.

'You're meant to be downstairs!' she hissed. 'The second show's about to start.'

The Doctor raised his eyebrows at me.

'*Fine*,' I said, as the girl pressed a carved wooden rose inlaid next to the fireplace, and a previously unnoticed door slid open in the wall. I followed her as we descended the steps to the corridors below.

Downstairs, everything was organised chaos. Thousands of identically clad wench-like girls were grabbing plates of hot meat and huge jugs of mead from a vast dispensing fountain – I rather liked that – in a complex but effective pattern.

Everything was hot and shouty, and I wandered into an endless kitchen full of workers of every conceivable stripe, hollering. They barely glanced up at me, and then I found a dressing room full of crying Valkyries, which led to an underground stables, full of pawing horses.

The girls asked me if I was Calinth's replacement and I said yes, and took the breastplate and the sword they gave me – it was a rather fine specimen – then I marched on, until I reached a side door marked 'Security', where I saw an empty stretcher.

'Excuse me,' I said, walking in. 'What's going on?'

'You can't be in here,' shouted someone.

'Really?' I said, fingering the sword. 'Well, tell me what's going on with Calinth and I'll leave quietly.'

A familiar furry figure stepped up, his whiskers twitching slightly.

'No, no, it's all right, Tullus,' he said. 'She's on our side.' He looked around. 'You've disconnected the cameras, right?'

'What's happening?'

Postumus looked crestfallen. 'It's the dimensional calibrator,' he said. 'Now somebody's messing with it.'

'Messing with it how?' I said.

'Well, it's carefully calculated, so everyone gets their Valhalla dining experience, whenever they want it. But someone's started folding the dimensions in. That poor girl was standing in a room that suddenly winked itself out of existence. She fell out of nothing.'

I blinked.

'She's going to be OK, though,' he added.

'And you don't know who would do that?'

The mouse called Tullus looked up. 'We love this place,' he said, and the others snuffled agreement.

'I need the Doctor,' I said.

134

I'd expected him to be doing what he usually did: making friends with everyone and becoming the centre of attention whilst pretending that sort of thing didn't matter to him.

Instead, he was sitting sulkily on the side by himself, pushing some food around his plate.

In front of the fire, an armoured chap with a huge glittering spear was roaring, 'So Odie, I said. So, Odie, let me tell you a thing or two about the bridge between the worlds. I mean, my bro and I got beef!' and the audience was either falling about laughing or hanging on to his every word.

'What's up with you?' I hissed.

'Well, he looks nothing like me, for starters,' said the Doctor crossly.

'Why would he?' I asked surprised.

'Oh, *no reason*,' he said. 'Just, you know. Mythological shapeshifter from ancient Earth history? Wears many faces? Plays tricks?'

I turned to him. 'That actor is meant to be playing *you*? *You're* Loki?'

'Credit where credit's due, that's all I'm saying. I was there. And *he's* a ham.'

'You're a ham,' I pointed out. 'Also he's very good-looking.'

'Do you really think so?' said the Doctor, brightening up.

'Anyway, that's not the point,' I said, and explained that someone had messed with the dimensional calibrator.

He turned ashen immediately and leapt to his feet.

'Is that bad?'

'Bad? It's. . . River, of course it's bad. It's like pulling a thread. . . you can't just tinker with a dimensional calibrator. . .'

And just as he said this, something started to shift. Just a very tiny amount, hardly at all. Blink and you'd miss. . . suddenly, there were two Lokis. And two tables. The great fire suddenly subdivided into two fires, catching a passing server, whose sleeve caught fire. She screamed.

Then there were more tables, and more, with people crowding out.

'We have to get them out!' shouted the Doctor, beating out the girl. 'It'll start to fold in on itself.'

Terrified staff were running in from secret doors all over the place, trying to get the crowds to muster and leave by the great doors.

I went to the great door. But as it opened I saw it opened not onto the outside, but instead into another great hall, with another Loki and another set of terrified people, trying to leave by another door, and yet another beyond. It had become an endless hall of mirrors.

Worse: the great fire that had caught the serving girl, had now caught the tapestries. The flames were ripping up the walls. Not just in our hall, but in every hall.

'It'll collapse in on itself,' shouted the Doctor, 'and leave nothing but the fire! We have to get these people out of here!'

The fire was licking at the straw roof of the great hall, even as the people were now cowering under the tables.

'Shield maiden,' said the Doctor, looking straight at me.

I looked back at him and nodded, and ran to the door. I pressed the carved wooden rose, and then we were down below, with staff running here and there in panic. We ran straight through the kitchen, where the mead was already beginning to bubble worryingly, and on to the dressing room.

'Sister Valkyries!' I shouted. The girls were cowering in the corner; their horses beyond whinnying and stamping in distress. The dimensional folding was happening here too; the stables went back and back and back.

'Now we go save them!' I shouted, holding up my sword.

They looked at me, astounded and terrified.

The Doctor didn't waste a moment, and swung himself onto the back of the nearest horse. I heard him whisper, 'What's your name? Oh, sorry, I forgot you're a robot.'

Then I followed suit. I turned to the girls. 'FOR WE ARE TRUE VALKYRIES,' I hollered at them, 'AND YOU WILL FOLLOW YOUR BRUNHILDE!'

And, astonishingly, they mounted their own horses and followed us.

Then we were off; clattering through the kitchen; bursting through the door into the great hall. The horses knew what they were programmed to do, and in that vast space, they took off, their wings flapping. It was the most astonishing feeling. I glanced over at the Doctor, who grinned back at me; he was enjoying it as much as I was.

We circled the hall, then he broke through the smouldering hay into the starry night beyond and I followed.

Below us the great palace of Valhalla was an endless city now; rooms upon rooms upon rooms; an Escher jumble of the near-infinite.

Except behind us, up flew the other Valkyries through the roof; bold and strong and fearless; and from every other roof in every other iteration flew a line of Valkyries too; and we all banked sharply and flew down, scooping up the people in our own version of the great hall; one by one, or two by two, or in the case of a particularly small family from Junveres, seventeen by seventeen; we lifted them onto the backs of our winged horses, flew them up through the flaming roof under the great white winter moon and set them down gently on the great golden fields of Freyr the harvest goddess, beneath the bright freezing stars.

Just as we rescued the very last of the people from the great hall, the Doctor shouted, and I raised my sword in the air for everyone to stop. There was a vast, teetering silence from the herd of horses in the sky; even the hordes of frightened people in Freyr's fields held their breath.

Then, with a huge creaking noise, one, then another, then another hall folded into itself completely, like a house of cards, one by one by one, until they had all collapsed; folded themselves up and completely disappeared, leaving only the bare ugly network of tunnels and subways of Asgard™ beneath.

The crowd cheered as we set down the last of the rescued and dismounted, but the Doctor had no time; he was scanning the faces.

'Who did this?' he demanded. '*Who?* Because people work really hard for their holidays, and you're just...

you're just spoiling everything.' He stalked the hordes. 'Have you any idea how much we need a holiday? I'm travelling the universe and she's in PRISON.'

Everyone stared at me and I pretended to be very busy and distracted.

'. . . and I bet you all have the same thing. Just one day. To get away from your normal routine. To remember how much you love your family. To escape that feeling that everything is collapsing around your feet. And then it collapsed around your feet. And I think somebody here is responsible. . .'

There was suddenly a bolting figure from the back; a bright flash of blue, taking off towards where the tunnels began.

We turned and ran, chasing it. So did Postumus, who had reappeared, and moved remarkably fast on those long limbs of his.

Beneath the tunnels, everything was dank and utilitarian. We followed some very swift running feet.

'This way!' shouted Postumus, whose ears were pricked up. We followed him, the pathway twisting and turning and getting deeper.

Suddenly I clanked against something, and I nearly tripped. My leg was caught. 'What's that?'

'Oh, yeah,' puffed Postumus. 'That's the monorail. For the transportation pods.'

'The *what*?' I said. But it was too late. Already, I could see a gleam of light ahead, as one of the little pods was heading straight for us.

'Get into the side, River!' shouted the Doctor.

But I had seen something – something just ahead.

'It's blue!' I shouted. 'Get the guy! He's blue!'

I couldn't move my leg. The train was coming closer and closer. It didn't appear to have a driver.

'Go on!' I shouted. 'Get him!'

But the Doctor stopped running and turned back towards me; they both did. And both Postumus and the Doctor instantly gave up their quarry and came towards me and, with an extremely ungracious 1-2-3 HUMPH, quickly pulled me out of my boots. The Doctor heaved me first and rolled with me to the left side; Postumus made a dive to the right and, to our utter horror, didn't make it in time.

The white pod rolled past and over him, and, just underneath it, we saw one little paw, lying limp on the rail.

We dived back down to the track. Postumus was lying, eyes shut. His legs were horribly mangled. I stroked his very soft fur. Then I looked up.

At the end of the passageway, there stood a tall blue, humanoid shape, outlined in the lights.

I leapt up and pulled out my sword. 'And now,' I shouted, 'I believe you harmed a friend of mine.'

I stalked up the tunnel, sword trained on his chest.

As I drew closer, however, I noticed something. The figure wasn't trying to escape or attack. And yes, it was tall: but it wasn't a man. It was an overgrown child; it was the teenager we had noticed earlier; his gadget dangling from his fingers. Also, he was crying.

'I didn't mean it,' he sobbed, his mouth a wobbly line. 'I didn't mean it, but...'

'I've got a pulse!' shouted the Doctor, as I led the boy back down the tunnel at the tip of my sword.

'And I've got a miscreant. Did you just perform mouth to mole?' I said.

'It's not so bad once you get used to it,' said the Doctor, wiping his lips.

Postumus's eyes began to flicker.

'What... what happened...?'

I stroked his nose. 'It's all right,' I said. 'You've hurt your legs. But we'll get help.'

He nodded. 'They won't hurt,' he whispered. 'Do you know, they're actually augmented legs.'

'I absolutely hadn't noticed,' I whispered back, and he smiled.

And then, thankfully, the ambulance arrived, and transported us back to the central base.

All the lights were on in the control room, screens showing a rapidly emptying park. Postumus was propped up. Caius was marching up and down in front of the boy, who was apparently called Tomith, and his quivering parents.

'What on earth were you thinking?' he was shouting. For something that looked like a beaver, he was actually quite scary. 'You killed people! You nearly killed my staff! You could have killed everyone in that hall.'

Tomith was staring at the ground, trembling. 'I didn't mean any harm.'

'Oh, you didn't mean any harm,' said Caius. 'You might have destroyed this place for ever, you know that?'

'I was just hacking. Your security systems are so simple.'

The bristles went up on the back of Caius's neck. 'They're the finest on the market today!'

'Well, they're still terrible,' said Tomith. 'But I didn't. . . I didn't realise that would happen if you messed with the dimensional calibrator.'

'A little knowledge,' said the Doctor.

'You know the sentencing in this part of the world for hacking?'

One of Tomith's triparents burst into tears.

Tomith trembled even harder. 'I'm so so sorry. I've got exams and everything back on Nurfer. I'm really, really sorry, Sir.'

'You'll be even more sorry when you're on Death Row.'

The parent now looked close to collapse.

Tears ran down Tomith's face. 'I only wanted to mess with it a bit.'

'Well, you messed with the wrong theme park.'

'How old are you?' said the Doctor.

'Fifteen,' said the boy, or that's what the TARDIS translated for me.

The Doctor raised his hands up. 'He's a child, Caius.'

'He's a criminal child.'

'If I were you, I'd give him a job.'

'What?!'

'Sort out your security breaches once and for all. Poacher turned gamekeeper. . . No offence,' said the Doctor, looking round at the assorted woodland animals. 'Because it seems to me, Caius, you need a new perspective.'

'But he's going to be prosecuted. . .'

'You have children, Caius?'

Caius shrugged. 'Yeah,' he said.

'And how do you think they're going to feel when their dad loses his job for letting his park be destroyed... *Or* perhaps it stood up to a major test incident. And learned how to pass it... to make it truly secure.'

'I could do that,' gulped Tomith. 'I could!'

One of the triparents nudged another. 'A job!' they said in astonishment.

The Doctor moved closer to Caius. 'Could you send one of your own children to their death? For breaking the rules?'

'They wouldn't do anything like this.'

'Is there anything they could do, Caius? That could make you send them to their deaths?'

There was a long silence in the room.

Then Caius waved his paws in a gesture of dismissal. 'Fine,' he said. 'Postumus, can you handle it? If I promote you to Head of Security?'

'When I get my new legs, I will,' said Postumus, looking delighted.

Tomith couldn't believe his luck. A parent started singing a Pharax song of profound gratitude that wasn't particularly welcome. And the Doctor gave Tomith a look.

'You channel those enormous brains,' he said severely. 'Don't you dare get in trouble again. Don't you dare let your parents down like that.'

'I won't,' stammered Tomith, in tears of relief now. 'I promise, I won't, Sir. I'm so sorry. I'm so, so sorry.'

And he broke down again, and the Doctor ruffled his hair.

Oh, and then it hit me like a rock in the guts.

Not that it was any business of mine. But that was what he would be like as a father.

And what do I know? Maybe he does it already. Maybe they're out there and he turns up every morning to breakfast. Maybe he zips back in time and tucks them in every single night, a little millisecond late here or there from some tight spot; different face sometimes; they never mind.

Maybe he's their funny uncle. Maybe they are legion, woven across the sky; or maybe he has peered into every dark corner of the universe and decided he could never be so cruel as to bring an innocent life into it.

Who knows, maybe some of them are mine.

Although you'd think he'd have mentioned it.

Outside, there was a small knot of disgruntled park visitors – everyone else had gone home, but they were still there, clamouring for compensation and calling it disgusting. Amongst them was the large lady, with little Mure, who was sitting on the ground, crying and wailing in utter exhaustion, ignored by his mum, who was shouting about her rights.

'River,' said the Doctor. 'Give me your sword.'

'No,' I said. 'I like it and I want to keep it.'

'Give it to me.'

I grudgingly handed it over, and he took off all but a tiny rounded nub at the end with the sonic. Then he programmed something into it and handed it back to the child. Now, the blunt-edged sword played its own fireworks. He gave it to Mure, who stopped crying and we headed on back to the gates.

'I'm just saying, I liked that sword,' I said.

'Sssh,' said the Doctor.

We got to the edge of the Rainbow Bridge. Everyone had finally left; we had the entire park to ourselves. The Doctor winked at something that must have been a camera, and suddenly, the night lifted entirely, and suddenly we were in a perfect, golden dawn, in a meadow, next to the empty bridge, wildflowers everywhere and the warm sun on our necks.

'Picnic?'

After we'd eaten, he lay back, sighing in contentment, his head in my lap, and started pointing out the inconsistencies in the sky system. I could have mentioned that he was criticising a replica of a wholly imaginary atmosphere, but I don't think he'd have cared.

Then he stopped in mid-flow and reached up, one of his fingers – they seem, through every iteration, to stay abnormally long; Time Lord fingers are always a dead giveaway – twirling up through the curls in my hair.

'What are you thinking about?' he said. 'You look sad. I hate sad. It makes me itchy.'

I looked down at him. 'I know,' I said, and I stroked his cheek. 'It's nothing.'

'But you should still tell me, River-Runs-Deep. Shouldn't you? Should you? Is this one of those things I always get wrong, like flowers are GOOD presents and trees are NOT GOOD presents? Mystery of the Universe right there.'

'Mystery of the Universe,' I said, breathing out and trying to let go of the idea of that extraordinary thing I yearned for; life that remakes life on and on and on.

That no matter what the science tells you, the fact that something alive can grow inside you, something brand new and unique – even though it is made of the same mix of stardust and honey and hope as everything else that ever lived – is a mystery; that every baby is a piece of magic.

'You don't believe in magic, do you?' I said, and he laughed.

'No!'

I shoved him off then and jumped up. 'Well, that's a shame, because the Great Wiagler is doing a private show for us in five minutes, if you wanted to catch it.'

'Ooh! I do!' he said, scrambling to his feet. We started off in the direction of the beehive meridians.

'Does he shoot fiery breaths across the sky?'

'He shoots fiery breaths across the sky.'

'Does he juggle dragon eggs?'

'Yes, but they're very ethically sourced.'

'Will he let me choose the cards? Because, I have a system, right. . .'

And we did have fun. It was brilliant. We laughed and ate far too much, and he didn't even moan too much about the food, and we stayed up too late and I danced with Postumus on his new legs at the woodland staff celebration party under the three sickle moons and the Northern lights; and he got me back last night just before they sounded the alarms, and I lay on my cold stone bunk alone and thought what a fun family day out Asgard™ might make or could have made or was, one day.

They say a psychopath cannot imagine the world any other way but their own. That their version of reality is the only one that matters to them.

They are so wrong about me.

All the Empty Towers

'"Kiss-me-quick-squeeze-me-slowly"?'

'Yes! Hilarious. See?'

'"Kiss. Me. Quick. . . Squeeze. Me. Slowly." Nope. Still nothing.'

'It's just a joke.'

'Is speed of central importance in these actions?'

Clara fixed the Doctor with a look, which he ignored as he placed the pink shiny metallic hat back down on the TARDIS console without trying it on.

'Fine, change the subject,' she said with a sigh.

'Shouldn't it be quick*ly*? Kiss me quick*ly*? Is it funny now?'

'Never mind.'

'*Kick* me quick. Now I can see how that might work. Kick me quick. . . appease me slowly.'

Clara marched across the console room, doing her best to keep calm.

'I just thought you might like to see where I'm from. That's all. My home. I thought you might like to visit it.'

Once upon a time, she thought bleakly, you would have. And we'd have had such a wonderful time. And you'd have loved that damn hat.

'A "black pool". Right. Good things very seldom come out of black pools in my experience. Oozing things do. Scuttling beastie type things.'

'Well, *I* did.'

'That's why you scuttle so much.'

'I do not *scuttle*! I...'

'Flounce?'

'*Glide!*' Clara tried again. 'We'll go up the tower! See the ballroom! And the illuminations! And I'll make you eat candyfloss!'

There was a very long pause. The Doctor's face was stern. Then he turned round, slowly.

'I love candyfloss.'

The TARDIS wheezed to a halt. Dressed in a black top and mini-skirt, Clara ran delightedly to the door.

'Home!' Then she turned round and regarded the Doctor. 'You'll have to take that coat off.'

The Doctor looked up, surprised. 'Well, I don't think so.'

'It's Blackpool. Nobody ever wears a coat.'

'Oh dear. A deal breaker.' He turned back towards the console display.

'You always get like this when you're doing something nice,' shouted Clara cheerily as she headed for the door. 'I just ignore it. Mind you,' she went on, almost to herself, 'Blackpool in November... maybe we can let you off just this once.'

Then she stepped out of the TARDIS into a steaming hot jungle.

The vines hung heavy in the trees, which were weighed down with strange brightly coloured fruits. The air was damp and sweet with the scent of rotting vegetation. Underfoot were fallen fronds and burst pomegranates, decaying where they lay.

'Oh no,' said Clara, looking round, her hands on her hips. 'This isn't Blackpool. Stupid TARDIS.'

The Doctor popped his head out of the door, then glanced back at the console readout. 'It most certainly is,' he said as he stepped out into the lush green landscape. 'Oh, it's lovely! You should have said!'

'No!' said Clara. 'This is a jungle! Blackpool has a Ferris wheel. And a beach! And. . .' She looked up. Overhead, the great wrought iron structure of the Blackpool Tower was slightly tilted. It had oxidised, and great vines twisted their way through the gaping holes in its structure. Brightly coloured birds swooped round the top. In front of them was what remained of the Golden Mile. Smashed lightbulbs crunched underfoot from the ruined illuminations; the promenade was completely overgrown, and high black waves lapped right across the cracked tramlines. In the distance, through the broken-down struts of the Big One rollercoaster, she saw, stilting along awkwardly –

'. . .*giraffes*?' Clara whipped round to face the Doctor. 'Giraffes? What's happened to my hometown?'

The Doctor took out his pocket watch. 'Oh. Yeah. Bit late.'

She glanced at the writhing greenery. 'Is this the trees doing a thing again?'

The Doctor shook his head sadly. ''Fraid not. This is here to stay. It's 2089. It's climate change. The real deal.

Looks like all those Bags for Life you bought didn't quite do the trick.'

Clara stepped forward, horrified. 'The Golden Mile, the sand. . . it was already eroding in my time, you could see it. But they built these sea defences. . .' She looked at them. The concrete barriers were overwhelmed with water; crumbled away.

Horrified, Clara started to run down the promenade, broken glass crunching under her feet. The pier sagged heavily into the high seas, bent and twisted into cruel shapes, dripping vines. Past the pier, a spit of black sand remained, in front of the ruins of the fish and chip shops; upturned plastic ice cream bins bobbing up and down in the water; a shipwrecked tram. She stopped and stared, mouth open.

Hurtling across the sand at full pelt, their heads and manes tossing in the warm wind, their hooves galloping in the rushing water, was a herd of wild donkeys. They looked beautiful and strange, outlined against the dark seas.

Clara's hand went to her mouth.

The Doctor came over, casually eating a handful of grapes that stained his mouth. 'This place is amazing. . . What?'

'The donkeys! They're running wild!'

'Beautiful. . .'

As they watched the animals gambolling in the surf, suddenly, as if out of nowhere, came a flashing, buzzing noise. A jagged silver disc, smaller than a frisbee, zipped through the sky, and embedded itself in the side of one of the donkeys, which immediately whinnied in distress and collapsed on the beach.

'Oh no!'

Clara darted across the sand towards it, as the herd left the creature behind. The wounded animal was tossing and writhing in pain, and she couldn't get close for the thrashing hooves.

'That projectile was about the size of a CD,' said the Doctor, coming up behind her. 'I wonder what it was. Simply Red? I mean, I can understand the urge to throw...'

The donkey was grunting and screeching as the Doctor moved closer, his face taking on an expression, Clara thought, rather gentler than the one he habitually wore when dealing with creatures on two legs.

'Sssh,' he said. He knelt down away from the animal's pistoning limbs, and put both hands either side of the donkey's head.

The flailing, terrified creature was immediately soothed at his touch, and quietened its terrible keening and thrashing.

'Sssh.'

The donkey and the Doctor regarded one another, as the Doctor very carefully and steadily, making no sudden movements, took one hand from the creature's head, and slowly pulled the jagged silver weapon from the donkey's side, hurling it away. Then, without breaking eye contact, he took out his sonic and quickly sealed and cauterised the wound.

The donkey's muzzle relaxed in the Doctor's hands, and it made a quiet braying.

'There, there.'

Clara looked around. She screwed up her eyes against the sun.

'Who did that? Who was it?'

Bang. The next silver disc missed the Doctor's boots by inches. He jumped up, patting the donkey briefly on its flank.

'Don't worry, Meghan. We'll get this sorted, OK?'

Pow!

The disc shot straight across the black sand. The sun poured through the canopy of overgrown bushes on the promenade, as Clara and the Doctor backed away rapidly towards the water.

'The donkey's called Meghan?'

'She's not called anything... Thought she might like Meghan.'

They splashed through the black water and crouched behind a twisted stanchion, as the Doctor pointed towards a distant window in an overgrown boarding house. A tumbled sign read 'The Arnold Guest House'; Clara remembered it well. It had already been nearly derelict when she was a girl.

Now, the jungle had grown straight through it. Thick vines had broken through the tiles of the roof, so it looked like the guest house had come down from the sky and landed on a tree, rather than the other way around. Every empty window frame was a mass of twisted greenery. In one of the upper windows, Clara suddenly caught sight of a flash of light; and in the next instant, a buzzing silver disc shot right over their heads.

The Doctor grabbed her by the hand and they splashed deeper backwards into the water under the eerie blackness of the skeletal pier. Clara blinked as, from the waves, a shoal of flying fish leapt up, their strange yellow webbed fins glinting in the spots of light; then they splashed back underwater.

'Whoa!'

Together they spied an abandoned pedalo; flotsam, bobbing underneath the pier. They glanced at one another.

'I don't think so,' said the Doctor.

'Pedalos are cool,' pleaded Clara. 'It'll be fun!'

The latest disc bounced off the top of the water.

'It's not a day for fun!' said the Doctor.

'Yes, well, that's becoming clear,' said Clara.

Instead, they waded across to the other side of the pier, out of range, then splashed full pelt over the esplanade wall that was covered in broken glass from the shattered lights. They ducked across the tramlines, faded and dull underwater. Then they circled round and backed up Pleasant Street, looking out for the sniper. Clara noticed in passing her old favourite chippie, but all she could smell now was thick green vegetation, heavy and exotic fruit.

The Doctor opened the rotting wooden back door of the Arnold with a swift kick.

'Hey!' he shouted loudly. 'Sniper boy! We're completely unarmed and you're playing "Now That's What I Call Chopping Up a Donkey Volume 1", so how about you come down and we have a wee chat about that?'

There was silence. The ancient carpet beneath their feet was brown and moist, but in here, amongst the damp creepers, Clara could still sense something of the many, many old breakfasts, the bacon and the sausage and over-stewed tea and HP sauce. She found it comforting.

There was no noise. The building was large, with many creaking, chipped old doors opening off a long corridor, covered in peeling fire exit signs.

'Third floor, fourth window from the left,' whispered the Doctor. They stopped and listened.

Suddenly, overhead, there came a footstep – steady, heavy in tread – then another.

'Come out, you big feartie!' shouted the Doctor

'What if he comes down and shoots us with his silver frisbee thing?'

'I'll talk him out of it with my friendly wit and charm.'

'So we're doomed, then.'

There was a creaking of a vine, and a large pineapple bounced down the stairs straight past them. Clara jumped, and glanced at the Doctor, whose face was impassive.

The footsteps continued slowly, and Clara found she was holding her breath.

'Hello?' she shouted. The staircase, wound around with vines, headed upwards into darkness.

The footsteps stopped over their heads. Then, very slowly, a foot appeared at the top of the twisted stairwell. It was wearing a very worn, grubby sheepskin slipper, over a pair of very baggy tan-coloured tights. The Doctor and Clara watched as another leg continued down, revealing a matching slipper: but the leg in this slipper was a skeletal steel.

'Are you going to shoot us?' said Clara, trying to sound brave.

'It's after 9 a.m.!' came a harsh metallic voice. 'No guests in the guest house after 9 a.m.!'

Clara backed away. The figure continued to descend. It was half a very old woman, swathed in layers of nighties and a huge filthy floral patterned housecoat. Ancient rollers were wrapped in thin dead wisps of hair, under a dirty headscarf. The other half of her face, where the wizened skin had been worn away, was metal.

The half-woman, half-machine brandished a large silver circular launcher at them.

'What is she?' asked Clara.

'Most horrifying creature in God's creation,' whispered the Doctor. 'A landlady!'

That got the half-woman's attention.

'No guests in the guest house after 9 a.m.!'

The Doctor moved forwards. 'I'm sorry to disturb you, madam. We were hoping to rent a room for the night?'

'Off-season! No guests in the guest house after 9 a.m.!'

She blinked very hard suddenly, looking slightly confused, and Clara wondered if she knew what she was.

'Where did everybody go?' asked Clara gently.

'Off-season! Off-season!' Her voice was sounding more robotic. She lifted up the blaster. 'No guests in the...'

Clara moved towards her.

'No, wait!' said the Doctor, trying to stop her. But Clara shook him off.

'Are you all right?' she asked gently. The woman's face suddenly looked more human than robot, and Clara felt very sorry for her.

The woman looked down. 'I don't like it when it gets dark,' she said. 'The animals make noises.'

'What are you doing shooting animals?' asked the Doctor in consternation.

The woman's face turned still and her voice took on a metallic tinge again. 'Got to have sausages for breakfast! Guests need sausages! Sausages and out by 9 a.m.! But you're not guests, are you? Are you sausages?'

The woman moved forward suddenly, incredibly swiftly, and opened her mouth. The scream, when it came, was horrifyingly loud.

'NO GUESTS!' she screamed, advancing with the blaster. 'NO GUESTS!!!!!'

The Doctor grabbed Clara by the hand and led her backwards towards the door.

'Wait!' wailed the half-woman.

'But she's. . .' said Clara, still stricken. There was a sudden whirring noise outside.

'Clara, she's *not* a confused old lady!' said the Doctor, furiously. 'Have you seen how they make sausages?'

They ran out of the old boarding house – but it was already too late. Four spaceships were hovering above the ground, surrounding them. They were small ships, open at the top, and in each was a young man or two, staring at them, laughing, pointing their blasters in their direction.

The spaceships were silver: pointed at the front, short range, nippy- looking things, and they bobbed strangely up and down in the air. They reminded Clara of something, but she couldn't think what.

'Hands up!' came a loud, entitled voice. The Doctor let out an irritated growl.

'Nice ships,' whispered Clara, putting up her hands.

'What!? They're all round. . . and slick, and aerodynamic-y,' said the Doctor in disgust.

A young man in a bright red jacket popped his head out of the top of one of the ships and waved his arm crossly. 'I say, what the ruddy hell are you doing in my hunt?'

'Your *what*?'

'My hunting grounds. It's clearly marked. All of the Pleasure Beach is a hunting ground.'

'It's a *what*?' said Clara again.

The man sighed. 'Oh lord, are you frightfully dim? My friend and I have hired out the Hunt. You're trespassing on my shoot.'

'Climate change drove people out... so they turned it into a hunting zone?' said Clara, incredulously.

'Well, you would keep electing those posh boys,' murmured the Doctor.

The man's lip curled. 'Anything that comes across our path is fair game, what?'

All his fellows laughed and passed a bottle amongst themselves, and one launched a silver disc straight up into the air. It caught the sun as it fell, slicing through the air. The man took a large swig of his own hip flask, and smiled unpleasantly.

'We were hoping to bag a big one today – it's my stag night.' He glanced at his fellows. 'Shall we bag an oik, boys?'

The other men laughed unpleasantly.

'Debag the oiks, more like!' squealed one excitedly. 'Let's go, Triss!'

The Doctor stepped forward, gripping his lapels. 'I don't think so.'

'Oh, it *talks*!' said Triss. 'Calm down, dear.'

The other men guffawed.

'You probably want to think very seriously about what you're doing here,' the Doctor went on.

Triss whirled round in his silver ship, his mouth slack and wide.

'No we *don't*!' he roared suddenly. 'We have to live in a world your generation ruined. We have to live in a world nobody your age "thought seriously about" at all. You left us with black sand and black water and black pools. And all we have left is a damn rare chance to have a little sport. And this is my stag night. And I shall have my sport, old man.'

He unleashed a disc that struck the Doctor's foot, and would have made anybody else jump.

'Hang on. . . Who on earth would marry *you*?' said Clara, stepping forward.

'I own the very last snow-topped mountain in Switzerland,' said the man called Triss. 'They're queuing up, I assure you.'

His friends laughed again. Triss looked down on Clara and the Doctor, a dangerous look on his face, and took another swig from his flask. 'The landlady wasn't expecting you,' he said. 'Which means *nobody* knows you're here. I wonder if you'll be missed?'

The others laughed. He raised his circular blaster. 'Three. . . two. . . one – tally ho!'

And one of the others blew a hunting horn.

The Doctor and Clara pounded down the esplanade and hurled themselves into the first building they came to, a huge old crumbling edifice of brown stone. They found themselves in a large ticket office with glass windows facing inside and out.

Clara looked around. 'Oh my god,' she said. 'This is the old circus! My nan brought me here!'

'What animals did they have?' said the Doctor.

'Oh, *now* you're interested in my childhood... Are they really trying to kill us?'

'*Hunting is a savage pleasure, and we are born to it,*' quoted the Doctor, then leapt forward and pulled Clara to the ground, as a jagged silver disc shot right through the rotten wood, embedding itself where her neck had been moments before.

The Doctor got up and pulled the disc out of the wall. It was incredibly sharp. Clara looked at him from the floor, her heart thudding in her chest. She looked around the ruined palace.

'Is this what happens? Is this it? Is this what happens to the town I was born in? To my home? To the world?'

The Doctor shrugged. 'It's not a fixed point in time, if that's what you mean.'

Clara's face brightened, a little, and she straightened up. 'Then that's good enough for me.'

She crept very carefully closer to the small window, and eyed up the little silver ships, buzzing and bouncing around the sky, the men boasting and shouting to one another.

'Is it just me, or is there something odd about those ships?' said Clara. 'They don't look like they're being steered properly, they just bump all over the place.'

'You're right,' said the Doctor, joining her. 'You'd expect them to move differently depending on who was driving them. But they don't. They all look the same. Like—'

'Like dodgem cars!' burst out Clara, suddenly. 'They wobble around each other like they're being really badly steered. Like dodgems!'

'But dodgems have an overhead power source.'

'I know.'

The Doctor held up his sonic and did some fast triangulation. 'If you connect up the angle of their aerials,' he said. 'You come back to the power source. . .' He followed the line with a long finger. Then he stopped and stabbed at the sky. 'It stops just overhead. What's overhead?'

'The tower,' gasped Clara, suddenly realising. 'We're at the bottom of the tower.'

'Hunting ships for hire,' said the Doctor. 'But attached.'

Triss suddenly stood up out of his ship again, laughing dangerously and pointing at them.

'Why is he laughing?' said Clara nervously.

'You know how I was asking what animals they had in the circus?' said the Doctor.

There was a sudden, low growl just outside the dusty space.

Clara jumped up. She could see the lion now, through a window in the office door. It was prowling through a great cavernous dusty space, with a wooden floor and old peeling posters for long-gone attractions. It was old, shaggy of mane, thin and hungry-looking, pacing the floor as if it didn't know what else to do; occasionally raising its great mangy head to sniff the air.

'Oh, my goodness,' said Clara. 'The circus! The zoo! The donkeys!'

'The hunt,' said the Doctor, opening his hands.

Clara glanced around the office desperately. There was a large works cupboard in the corner. As she opened it, a harsh hot wind blew down into the room, and a rattling noise filled their ears. The large space was completely filled with rubble.

'What's that?'

'Lift shaft,' said the Doctor. It was full of collapsed metal equipment. 'Can you climb it?'

Outside the office on one side, the lion threw back its ancient head and roared. On the other, another disc smashed the one remaining glass window, and Clara caught a glimpse of flashing silver.

Clara glanced at the lion and back at the Doctor. 'You know, he reminds me of someone.'

'Up!' said the Doctor sharply, as Clara pulled herself onto the oily metal chain.

They managed to climb two floors up the lift shaft before it became impassably blocked by machinery.

'There must be another lift,' said the Doctor.

Clara pushed up the hatch, and they both leapt out to run across the floor.

'Careful,' shouted the Doctor. 'It might be rotten.'

But Clara had made it as far as the middle of the floor, then stopped stock still.

The red velvet curtains bloomed with flowers of rot. The famous Wurlitzer organ lay in pieces, scattered amongst the vines that trailed across the famous sprung wooden dance floor; the gilded balconies crushed and collapsed one on top of the other.

'The tower ballroom,' said Clara reverently.

The Doctor had made it to the end of the floor already, and was opening up the opposite shaft with his sonic. 'Come on, Clara!'

'I always. . . when I was a little girl I was too shy. But I always wanted to dance on this floor. I always dreamed of it. Of coming back here one day. . .'

'You can't go home again,' the Doctor said. 'But you can get shot at by a bunch of overbred chin-free maniacs, if that helps.'

Clara wasn't listening; she was caught in a spell. She moved a step across the floor, then another, then looked up at him. 'Can you dance?'

The Doctor paused in exasperation. 'No, of course I can't dance! Come on, get climbing!'

'Never mind,' said Clara, sadly, as she followed him out and up.

The exterior lifts had long collapsed to the bottom, and the only thing to be done was to climb up and out, scaling the struts of the tower itself, hand over hand. It was frightening and exhausting, as they got higher and higher, and Clara looked out over the black water as far as she could see, and down, over her ruined town; and across, to where she saw great tall electrified fences, wild animals roaming the abandoned streets, the endless jungle and great lakes beyond, and above, a thick blanket of cloud, keeping in the oppressive heat, the sun blazing just beyond.

A hot wind swayed the tower, and the Doctor's foot slipped, but he managed to grab back on. The noise, however, startled a great company of parrots, who rose in the air, squawking wildly, and the Doctor and Clara heard the noise of the hunting horn, as the birds attracted the silver ships, which came rushing up towards them, bumping each other in their hurry. They felled a couple of the beautiful birds, but their real target was the Doctor and Clara themselves, who ducked underneath to attempt the far more difficult job of climbing up the inside. After two agonising floors of this, they reached a small platform with a service ladder, and started to move at full tilt, as the noise of connecting discs jarred their way up the metal structure.

They reached the trap door to the top viewing platform just in time, as one disc sliced through a cable, and an entire section of the ladder peeled off the side of the building and clanged its way a hundred metres below, smashing through the ballroom roof.

They found themselves in a high room lined with heavy glass that hadn't yet cracked: for the first time since they'd landed, Clara realised, there was power on. The room hummed with it. There was a central console with a large connecting wire that shot straight through the ceiling – the aerial.

The Doctor ran to the computer.

As soon as he touched the keyboard, immediately the alarm went off:

'NO GUESTS! NO GUESTS! NO GUESTS!!'

And from the dim shadows in the tiny control room at the top of the Blackpool Tower appeared another hideous half old lady, half robot; this one in a huge floral day dress covered in a stiff blue nylon tabard. Her face was more metal than the other's; the little skin left on it was dried and fraying off, like old leather.

'Sausages!' it said, starting to slowly raise its hand with the circular launcher. The silver pods surrounded the glass control room, buzzing back and forth and laughing. One was filming from a tiny device.

'Now that,' said the Doctor, typing furiously, 'would be a terrible last word to hear, wouldn't it? I mean, even "blood sausage" might have worked a bit better.'

He continued working feverishly on the console as the robot landlady advanced despite Clara's best efforts to kick at her swollen ankles in the sheepskin slippers.

'Doctor!'

Clara was back to back with the Doctor now, looking over his shoulder.

'Leave me alone,' said the Doctor, huffing in frustration. 'I need to do this. . . stupid computer. . .'

'Yeah I know,' shrieked Clara, as the hand rose higher and the scent of old breakfasts and popcorn and Rothmans filled the space. 'But you've left the Caps Lock on.'

'Oh yeah,' said the Doctor tutting. He typed some more, and suddenly the humming noise stopped, and the robot landlady abruptly powered down and collapsed onto the floor.

Clara let out a sigh of relief that turned to a yell of fright – as she saw through the glass walls the four silver pods surrounding them lurch, and then, suddenly, drop out of the sky.

'They're falling!'

The Doctor paused. For a barely an instant.

Then, with a sigh, he took out his screwdriver and planted it into the circuit, where it connected up the overhead power again.

'I think I've had a fall,' said the woman, querulously.

Clara looked at the Doctor, who shook his head tersely, typing with one hand. Instead, she peered out of the windows. The silver ships had juddered to a halt, and now were descending slowly and gracefully, round and round the tower, like a fairground ride, until they gently reached the ground and came to a halt. The lion leapt out of the booking office window to have a sniff about. The men's bravado did not extend to them getting out of their pods.

The Doctor complained about his burnt-out screwdriver all the way back down the endless climb and halfway across the ballroom.

Clara took one last look around. 'So no one will ever come here again?'

'I've sealed the fences and put in a skynet,' said the Doctor. 'These hunting grounds are closed.'

'I could never come back here anyway,' said Clara with a shudder, looking at the thick dust covered in their footprints. Motes floated in the air, lit by the hole in the ceiling that let in the sunlight, the whirling ghosts of dancers forever departed.

'Things decay,' said the Doctor. 'But remember, Clara, this isn't a fixed point. It doesn't have to be like this.'

Clara nodded glumly as they crossed the once pristine floor.

The Doctor looked at her stricken face. 'So maybe I do dance,' he said quietly. 'A bit.'

She looked at him.

'Obviously,' said the Doctor. 'You don't infiltrate the deadly French court without mastery of the gavotte.'

'The gavotte?' said Clara. 'Is that the only dance you can do?'

'No,' said the Doctor. 'Also, the quadrille. Take it or leave it.'

He knocked his blackened screwdriver several times hard against his boot, until it emitted a tiny peep and beam of light, and directed it towards what was left of the organ, which started up, creakily, painfully, its old programme, a very slow, mournful version of 'We Do Like to Be Beside the Seaside' in a minor key.

Clara put on her bravest smile as he reached for her hand.

The lion had long gone by the time they got down to street level and marched the chastened men to the perimeter fence. The Doctor saw Clara desperate to ask questions, and halted her with a look.

'Don't,' he warned gently. 'And you,' he said to Triss. 'If I hear of you treating your wife with a fraction of the contempt with which you treat the rest of creation – and I hear everything – I will happily bounce you off that tower myself, do I make myself understood?'

'Yes, sir.'

'Good boy. You can go.'

They stood on the beach, throwing pebbles in the water. The Doctor looked at Clara. 'You need to work harder in your own time, don't you think? Educate all those millions of children of yours? It's not fixed... yet.'

Clara nodded. Then she looked up at him. 'You do know they're not actually my children? I just teach them?'

The Doctor ignored her, and spoke on, gazing out at the sea.

Suddenly he was almost knocked into the surf by a donkey launching itself on him, licking his face like an overgrown dog.

'Hey!' he said. 'Hey, Meghan! How are you? How are you, girl? There you are.' He scratched behind her ears and she rubbed her head against him adoringly. Then she got down on all fours.

'Oh no,' said the Doctor. 'No. No. Definitely not.'

Clara smiled. 'I think she wants to. You should roll up the bottom of your trousers so you don't get wet.'

The Doctor gave her a look.

'Ooh!' She felt into her pocket and pulled out the pink plastic hat she'd grabbed from the console. 'And here. Stick this on!'

'No hats!'

'Stick it on!' She reached up and put it on for him.

'I don't want. . .' Meghan had already nudged herself underneath him, and got to her feet, lifting him up. 'I don't. . .'

But it was too late. Donkey and Time Lord were already proceeding at a stately pace through the shallow waters against the twisted wreckage of the pier. Clara, giggling, watched them splashing away in the light of the huge pink setting sun, as the Doctor gently rubbed the donkey's ears and, when he thought he was unobserved, planted a very quick kiss on the animal's head.

A Long Way Down

The TARDIS turning upside down was unexpected. Immediately a growly voice echoed around its walls. 'Clara, what are you doing?' 'Clara, what are you doing?' 'Clara, what are you doing?' 'Clara, what are you doing?'

Clara had been buried in lost scrolls in the South Library, where the light was the gold of Alexandria. The TARDIS-given ability to read in any language sometimes seemed to her as wondrous as any galaxy they could visit. She looked up from the floor, gathering the scrolls.

'What was that? Why did we loop the loop?'

'Small asteroid disturbance.'

'Asteroids can't do that to the TARDIS!'

There was a pause.

'Do you need help?' Clara asked tentatively.

'NO!'

There came a longer pause.

'Maybe.'

Clara entered the console room. To her surprise, the TARDIS door was open. Outside, a spiral galaxy floated like a jewelled shell. They were balanced on the tip of the atmosphere of a large brown planet. She moved forward carefully.

'Where *are* you?'

Even protected by the TARDIS's own atmosphere, she could feel the VAST emptiness of space.

'Why isn't the force field on?'

The voice resounded around the room.

'Because force fields are for custard-loving poltroons... and also I was just about to put it on when the asteroid hit...'

She dashed to the console – but it was too late. Through the door, she could just make out a tiny figure plummeting below her, flipping around, head over heels. Beneath him was something that looked like... a window box.

'YOU DIDN'T...'

'It could happen to anyone.'

'But window boxes are really UNCOOL! And surprisingly suburban.'

'I like them.'

'You've had thousands of people in this thing and nobody's ever fallen out before.'

'Not by *accident*.'

Clara looked around. The TARDIS was just under orbiting height at the very tip of the atmosphere of the desolate-looking planet. They were miles up. But at TERMINAL VELOCITY...

'Right, we're coming to get you... Aren't you cold?'

'No.'

Clara raised her eyebrows. 'You sound cold.'

'Actually, I'm boiling hot with embarrassment at the stupidity of your question.'

'Didn't you once tell me you used to have a scarf?'

'It LOOKED STUPID.'

'How long can you breathe for?'

'Oh, long enough to feel the annihilating pain of impact, don't worry.'

Clara got up and headed to the console. 'Can you set a quick trajectory for – you know, just beneath him?'

The TARDIS wheezed unenthusiastically.

'Sorry. *Please*,' said Clara. 'But if we're twelve miles above this planet, that gives us about…six minutes? So shall we get moving?'

The TARDIS's time motors fired up.

'No! It's pointless going back in time, because if we miss him we'll create a right mess. Just go down! Like a normal ship!'

The TARDIS stubbornly refused to move. Clara sighed and looked at her watch.

'This isn't a time problem! Except we don't have much. So just go down – really, really fast. Please?'

But the motors were already wheezing. The TARDIS shimmered, then reappeared, next to another TARDIS. Clara looked out of the first TARDIS just in time to see the Doctor, holding what appeared to be a window box full of delphiniums, leaning curiously out of the second door.

'Stop!' she shouted.

'What?' he shouted, twisting back - just as the asteroid flipped the TARDIS again, causing him to fall.

'Nooo!'

'Clara, what are you *doing*?' came a fading voice as he dropped once more down through the top atmospheric layers.

'So I'm still just *plummeting* down here to an early grave quite happily,' came the first Doctor's voice. 'Not *that* early, to be fair.'

'Oh no!' said Clara. She ran to the console.

'SEE!' she said. 'Messing about in time, nothing but trouble. Go and rescue both of them, and sort this out. IN SPACE.'

The TARDIS ignored her completely, and started once more to remove itself in time. Clara lunged for the handle, but could only move it halfway. Together, they tumbled over, dematerialising and rematerialising at a rate, lurching from side to side. Clara kept a tight grip on the handle, staring beyond the door. She caught sight of yet another Doctor, falling, his coat billowing behind him, and another TARDIS, hurtling round and round; presumably them from several instants before. She let go of the console and rushed to the door, popping her head out then pulling back in sharpish, only just avoiding getting knocked out as several boxes of delphiniums came hurtling past.

'Only,' came the deep tones, 'I can start making out certain topographical features. Like fifteen tiny pebbles and a mouse's back garden. But don't worry about me.'

'THE TARDIS WON'T BEHAVE,' shouted Clara in desperation. 'It won't do what it's told.'

They lurched diagonally several hundred feet.

'What, it isn't doing anything?'

'It is, but it's doing the wrong thing!'

The TARDIS continued to dematerialise and rematerialise. Now there were over twenty TARDISes hurtling through the air; Doctors were falling like raindrops.

Clara glanced down at her hands. She was still carrying one of the scrolls of Alexandria. Desperately, she hurled it out of the door.

'Can you catch that scroll?'

'What, in case I need something to *read*?'

The TARDIS lurched and whirled on, and suddenly the sky was filled with dancing, wheeling TARDISes, tumbling flowers, falling Doctors, passing asteroids and hundreds and hundreds of flut-tering scrolls. Clara saw herself fall straight past, like Alice, a surprised look on her face.

'Oh NO!' she said, banging her fists on the console. 'Why? Why are you doing this?'

The TARDIS jumped another millisecond. Clara pushed down again on the lever but the gears ground together. It let out a deep noise and descended a little. Not fast enough. Nowhere near fast enough.

'The nice thing about certain death this way,' came the Doctor's voice inside the TARDIS, 'is it's been really good fun having a bit of a fly before I went. Always wanted to fly. As long as I don't dwell on what's approaching in forty seconds' time, this is actually delightful.'

'Clara what are you doing?' The voice was now a chorus. 'Clara, what are you doing?' 'Clara, what are you doing?' 'Clara, what are you doing?' 'Clara, what are you doing?'

Clara jumped up on the console so she could have more traction on the lever, pressing her entire weight down on it.

'GET DOWN!!!!!!'

Something gave, and the lever pulled down all the way, and suddenly the TARDIS was dropping like a plummeting lift. She tried to steer, but it was impossible. She lost her balance and tumbled back, but fell and rolled across the ground to the open door. Then she stuck out her hand and caught a passing scroll. The ground was coming up fast to meet them, as they dropped past all the other TARDISes and other Doctors. She couldn't think about them. She could only think about hers. They were getting closer. The ground now filled her vision beneath her, brown, vast, and very very solid. They were too late.

'Spread yourself out!' she shouted down. 'Spread yourself out!!'

She turned off the force field, then – as soon as she spotted him skydiving, his coat billowing in the wind – she stood up, braced herself in the TARDIS doors, and dived out. She did not dare look up, but concentrated entirely on making herself as streamlined as possible, hurtling like an arrow through the sky to reach him. She grabbed his coat as they tumbled around together towards the earth, at first fumbling, and then holding on, and managed to unfurl the scroll to form a canopy above their heads as he looked at it, and said, 'Seriously?' And then, for the first time, he saw above him, saw what was raining down on top of them, and his mouth fell open.

BANG the first of the window boxes hit the ground, as the makeshift parachute slowed their descent hardly at all.

BANG another as they approached, too fast, holding each other tightly.

BANG more flowers, and more, and then they were bracing, bracing for impact, and Clara found herself facing upwards – as everything in the sky suddenly vanished and only they were still falling, but the landscape did not change and they did not hit the ground; and instead they found themselves suspended, momentarily, for the longest second, in mid-air. Then they broke through again, and fell ten feet, landing gently in a huge soft mound of delphiniums.

'She wove us a time field. She just needed all the extra bits of seconds to fit them in to break our fall.'

'Why not just come and get you?'

'And bump me into a spaceship? Have you *seen* the crystal room? Ouch. Not that I would have felt the pain, obviously. I eat pain for breakfast. Pain, and Frosties.'

'Why wouldn't she listen to me?'

'Why wouldn't you listen to her?'

Clara sighed. 'She won't talk to me.'

The Doctor looked at the console. 'No,' he said. 'She has things slightly the wrong way round. She thinks... she thinks whenever the really bad things happen, you're always there. I think she is having some issues with cause and effect. Order of. Time traveller problems.' He patted the TARDIS affectionately.

'Why would she think that?' Clara asked.

The Doctor paused, and then he lied. 'I don't know.'

Clara looked around, and sighed. 'You know,' she said. 'Sometimes I'm not sure you really need me here.'

The Doctor fixed her with a look.

'But you were there for me anyway.'

She nodded. 'Always.' And she turned away.

And as she did so, she said to herself, 'Clara. What are you doing?'

Acknowledgements

Deep and heartfelt thanks to: Albert DePetrillo, Justin Richards, Steve Cole, Jake Lingwood, Tessa Henderson, Paul Cornell, Gareth Roberts, James Goss, Matt Fitton, Matthew Sweet, Tom Spilsbury, Peter Ware, Jamie Mathieson, Pete Harness, Sarah Dollard, Isabel Hayman-Brown and all lovely Whovians everywhere.

Author Biography

Jenny T. Colgan has written numerous bestselling novels as Jenny Colgan, which have sold over 2.5 million copies worldwide, been translated into 25 languages, and won both the Melissa Nathan Award and Romantic Novel of the Year 2013. Aged 11, she won a national fan competition to meet the Doctor and was mistaken for a boy by Peter Davison.